Edgy People

stories

Barb Nobel

Library and Archives Canada Cataloguing in Publication

Nobel, Barb, 1948-, author
    Edgy people : stories / Barb Nobel. -- First edition.

Issued in print and electronic formats.
ISBN 978-1-927882-34-4 (softcover).--ISBN 978-1-927882-35-1
(Kindle).--ISBN 978-1-927882-36-8 (EPUB)

    I. Title.
PS8627.O185E34 2018   C813'.6   C2018-904477-2
                                           C2018-904478-0

For Iain

Contents

Tree Hugger

BILLY IS A BIG MAN, six-two at least. He stands under the red maple and looks at me. I'm up on the ladder, painting the house. I know I shouldn't have worn these shorts, but the day promised to be a scorcher. So far, the radio says, it's the hottest summer in eight years, and I'll be dammed if I'm going to sweat to death at work. I already sweat to death in that little shitbox trailer I live in. Billy makes no secret that he's looking at my ass, gazing with his mouth half open like an idiot.

Billy's a contractor, he builds houses. The houses are all finished in gorgeous velvet wallpapers, which cover a lot of faults, and fancy fixtures in the bathrooms, which somehow fool people into thinking they are getting a good deal. Then he pays me slave wages to paint the outside. Seaside blue is what I'm painting this place, with white trim, and I got to admit it doesn't look bad. I wouldn't mind living in one of Billy's houses. Even with all their faults, they beat what I'm living in now.

"Hey Terri, how's that painting coming?" Billy yells up.

Idiot. "You're looking at it, you tell me," I yell down.

"Come down for lunch," Billy yells up.

I do.

I park my butt under the maple tree, which provides a surprising amount of shade, and pull out my lunch, a peanut butter sandwich and an apple.

"Hey Billy," I say, "I gotta leave early today. I got a parent-teacher meeting at the school."

"Kevin in trouble again?"

I kick myself that I ever let him know how much trouble that kid was giving me. Last time I had trouble with Kevin, Billy offered to act as a father figure to the kid, seeing as how my old man left when the kid was three. I wanted to suggest to him that he act as a father figure to his own kids, but my friends always tell me I've got a big mouth, so instead I just told him my brother was acting as the father figure, and it didn't make any sense to get the kid more confused.

Billy pushes his cap back, exposing the white skin on his forehead.

"Wanna ask you something, Terri," he says.

"Sure Billy," I say all innocent, although I have a pretty good idea what's coming.

"You're an attractive woman, Terri. I been watching you for a while. Like you to share my pillow."

It isn't that Billy isn't a good looking man, and he's no drinker, but he is married with two kids.

"Can't do that, Billy. You're a married man," I say.

Billy takes off his cap and scratches his crew-cut.

"Well now, don't worry about that. I'll handle that part of it," he says.

"No Billy."

I gaze up through the branches of that maple tree. I do adore that tree. Living in a trailer park you get kind of sentimental about stuff like flowers and trees—things you never notice when you have them around.

"Beautiful tree," I say, because I got to say something to break the silence and lead the conversation away, and help the man forget that his ego's just been hurt.

"Yeah", Billy says. "I don't understand what the problem is, Terri. Everyone cheats on his wife. Jimmy cheated on you."

I know Jimmy cheated on me, but it's a done thing now, and I don't appreciate the reminder. This conversation isn't going the way I want it to.

"Sure could use a tree like this where I live," I say. "Would really provide some shade over the trailer. Gets up to ninety in there some days. Tree like this would make a big difference."

"Sure, Terri," says Billy.

He opens a new package of Players, offers me one, and studies me.

"Yup, sure could use a tree like this one," I babble.

Billy mumbles something about getting back to work, replaces his cap, and strolls over to his truck. I sigh, climb the ladder again. Stupid move. I should have waited. I can feel Billy looking at me through the truck windshield. If I didn't need the money, I would dump this job in a minute, but the support cheques don't stretch far these days. I know I'll finish this job, and take on the next one if he asks me to.

On Friday, the job is finished, and on Monday, while I'm getting Kevin ready for school, I hear this rumbling. Something's always happening in this trailer park, so I don't even bother looking out the window. But when I shoo Kevin out the door – there it is. The tree, I mean. The maple tree from the new house. Roots and all. It's on top of a huge truck-like vehicle, and one man is directing this vehicle through the maze of trailers with their temporary laundry lines, and the plastic ride-on toys that seem to belong to any kid who gets on them. I feel like someone pushed all the air out of my lungs, and I know I'm catching flies.

"You Terri?" hollers the man directing the truck.

He comes over and shows me where he's putting the tree. I'm still catching flies. I didn't know they could transplant full grown trees. I think there must be a mistake, but this man has a work order signed by Billy. I can't even imagine what it costs to move a whole tree, and when I ask, the man shakes his head like he doesn't believe it himself, and tells me I don't want to know. He also tells me to water it well for the first couple of months, because it's gonna be under stress, and don't be alarmed if it's leaves turn red earlier than usual in the fall, because that's how trees react to stress. He tells me all this twice to make sure I got it. By this time old Mr. McCracken is peering through his curtains. Then the machine starts pounding out a hole, and it's like when my parents had the well dug. I go into the trailer and think about what's happening. I know Billy isn't doing this for free. I know what he's going to ask next. First I decide to run out there and stop the work, but I don't know if the men would listen to me. They got a work order from Billy. I could order them off my property, threaten to call the police. Wouldn't the neighbours love that scene! They've already got me branded a slut because I'm a single parent. What would happen to the tree if I make them get it off my land? The thing might die waiting for Billy to tell the men what to do next. I decide that getting that tree doesn't oblige me to anything, no matter what Billy thinks. Then I decide that maybe I could, just once. Then I go against that. Billy is still a married man, and he shouldn't think he can buy me with a tree, no matter how expensive it is. I get up and look out the front window and see the hole is getting bigger and bigger. If I'm going to do anything, I'd better do it now. So I call Fay and tell her what's going on. Fay laughs and laughs. At first I'm upset, but then I see the funny side of it, and start to laugh too.

"Listen," Fay says on the phone, this doesn't oblige you to anything."

And we laugh some more.

We decide to meet at The Lonely Texan on Saturday and discuss it over a beer.

I look out the window again. The hole is gigantic. I call my mum if she can stay with Kevin Saturday night. She's okay with that.

When I get to The Lonely Texan I can see Fay's been there a while. She's wearing her tightest blue jeans and her red heels, and a fake cowboy is buying her beers. By the way she hollers "T-resa" across the room I know she hasn't been refusing the cowboy's offerings. I settle down with Fay and the cowboy, who is none too happy about me appearing on the scene. We're there about an hour when Billy walks in. He grabs a Blue, pulls a chair up to the table, and says hi. He asks me how I like the tree and I tell him just fine. When the lights go up Billy digs in his pocket for his keys and waggles his eyebrows at me, but I got my mind made up.

"No," I tell him. "You can't follow me home, you can't come in for a coffee, you can't stay the night."

Fay isn't helping. She's practically falling off her chair laughing. "Should've bought her beers instead of a tree," she shrieks.

"Come on Fay," I say, "I'm taking you home. I'll bring you back for your car in the morning. If it's hot we'll have a few beers under my tree first."

For once, she doesn't argue. The fake cowboy watches us leave. He knows he's wasted his money. Billy watches us, too. He knows he's wasted his money.

In the car Fay and I giggle all the way to her place, and then I giggle all the way to my place.

Wednesday morning, all hell breaks loose. I've just sent Kevin off to school when Billy pulls up in his truck. He gets out and reaches into the flatbed and hauls out a chain saw. I hightail it back outside and plant myself in front of the tree. Billy yanks the cord on the chain saw and it roars to life.

"Move," he says.

"I'm not moving," I say. From the corner of my eye I can see old Mr. McCracken's curtain flutter.

"Move," says Billy.

"No."

Mr. McCracken comes out on his trailer steps. "It's on her land," he says. He holds the phone receiver in his hand, the cord stretched out behind him into the trailer.

"Move."

Mr. McCracken hollers over that he's calling the police. Billy hesitates. Police reports wouldn't be good for business. Billy makes a decision, tosses the chain saw back into the flatbed, yells "You haven't heard the last of me" threats over his shoulder, throws himself into the cab, and roars off. It's the first time I've heard Billy gun that motor.

"Care for some coffee, Mr. McCracken?" I say, unfolding two lawn chairs and putting them under the tree.

"I'll bring the biscuits," Mr. McCracken says.

After this I don't get any more jobs from Billy, but that's okay because I got on the production line at Alcan, and I'm making decent money now.

The leaves are off the tree when I hear that Billy's moved out to the yukon, and a few weeks later I get a letter from him. It sounds like he's still pretty mad because his whole letter is about what an ignorant bitch I am, only he spells 'ignorant' wrong.

It's summer again and that tree is thriving. Those men certainly did a great transplant job. Fay and I, and sometimes Mr. McCracken if we're only drinking coffee, sit out there. And Fay says, "Terri, this is the first time that big mouth of yours got you somewhere, but this one time should last a lifetime."

And Fay and I and Mr. McCracken laugh like fools.

The Paper Mache Project

I'VE BEEN DOING PAPER MACHE for more than 50 years now. I took it up when I was a teenager, and lonely on a Saturday night. I was kind of a gawky teen, and spent most Saturday evenings sitting at home with my parents. I met Ed when I was about 26, and he was the first man to show an interest in me, so of course I married him when he asked. Like they said then, any man is better than no man. All the same, he turned out better than most.

Paper Mache is fairly simple, and cheap too. All you need is a form and lots of newspapers. I frequently use a balloon for the form, and then you pop the balloon and remove it when the paper is dry and hard. A large balloon, a small balloon, a couple Dixie cups for the legs, and you've got a pig in the making. Sometimes I built a form out of wire, twist ties, something like that.

I've done a lot of Paper Mache projects, but this is certainly the most ambitious one I've tackled. I'm going to need all those newspapers I've saved. But at least I've got a readymade form.

Ed always nagged at me about the newspapers, saying they were a fire hazard, but after a while I found that if I put them in the basement Ed didn't bother.

When we first got married Ed made fun of me for my craft, and I felt bad, but I told him that it was no worse than watching grown men chase a puck around the ice. All in all though, we got on fairly well. I miss him most at dinner, when we always had a civilized conversation about a new book, or about what was happening in the world.

Right now I'm busy ripping the strips off the newspapers. The strips are really long, which is what I need. Newspapers are dirty, and my hands are black when the Meals on Wheels lady knocks on the door. She remarks on the colour of my hands, and I tell her why I look so dirty. Lillian is her name. She asks after Ed, and I tell her that Ed is resting; he doesn't feel so well today. Lillian asks if Ed needs to go to the clinic, and can she call a volunteer driver. I assure her that it's just a cold, and take the two meals from her. I know I should probably tell her she only needs to bring one meal now, but instead I put the second meal in the fridge for dinner. I don't mind leftovers, and it saves me from having to eat jam sandwiches with tea for dinner.

This evening I'll get everything ready to make the adhesive that holds the strips of paper on the form. Ed use to claim it smelled bad. I never smelled anything, but to keep the peace I would do the preparation in the basement. Now I don't need to worry. I can do the prep work in the kitchen.

Of course when Beatrice and David were young I couldn't work at my art, I didn't have the time, but when they were both in school I took it up again.

Once, I sat Ed down and explained that Paper Mache was an art practiced in ancient Egypt and was used to make death masks. And that it was used later on in Europe to make ornamental trays, and other decorations. Then I made him a small box for his cufflinks. Ed was a real fan of maps, and I papered the box with maps. It turned out really nice, and Ed quite liked it. He gave it a place of honour on our dresser, and when cufflinks went out of fashion, he used it for small change. I miss seeing him drop his quarters and dimes into that old box, the last thing he did before changing for bed.

I measure the flour and water for the adhesive, and then Beatrice calls at 8 p.m. She used to call later but I let her know that I retire about 8:30 now, so she calls promptly at eight every Tuesday, Thursday, and Sunday. We talk about the weather, and what I'm having for dinner (I lie a bit here) and then she asks to speak to her Dad, and I tell her Ed is sleeping.

On Friday morning after breakfast I make the adhesive, and start on my project. I admit that this is an art that can be messy, and you should lay plastic down to protect any surfaces.

I use to make piñatas for the kids birthday parties, till they got to be about 11 or 12. The piñatas were a real hit at the parties, and I made a variety of shapes. Some of them were quite large, but of course none of them as big as the project I'm currently working on.

By 10 a.m. Friday morning I'm working in the bedroom, and the bed is getting really messy. This is a more complex project than I thought it would be. It's hard to get the newspaper strips to go on smooth. I want it to look good of course, but there are more lumps and bumps than I'm used to. I'll probably have to sleep in one of the kid's bedrooms tonight.

Lillian comes about 11:30, and when I open the door she steps back a bit. Then she asks me what that awful smell is. I tell her that it's the paste for my Paper Mache, but I can see she doesn't believe me. She says she thought the paste was just made from flour and water, and insists that it smells more like something died, maybe a rat or a racoon in the attic. I insist it's the paste that smells so bad. Lillian asks after Ed, and I tell her his cold is getting better, but he's still resting. Then she asks if she can talk to him, give him get well wishes, and I'm starting to get annoyed. Finally Lillian gets the message, hands me the two meals, and leaves. I know I won't have to worry about her till Monday. They don't deliver on the weekends, so I won't be interrupted.

If I don't take too many breaks I can do the first newspaper layer today, and the second on Saturday. Hopefully I won't need a third layer, but if I do, I can do that on Sunday.

By Monday the smell shouldn't be so bad. But I'll have to make up more excuses as to why Lillian can't see Ed. Maybe it would make sense to just cancel Meals on Wheels. Well, I'll have to think about that. I don't really want to start cooking again.

I'll have to make up excuses for Beatrice as well, to explain why she can't talk to her dad when she telephones.

Well, Ed was always a man of few words, now he's a man of no words.

On Saturday I have got the second layer of paper on, and Ed is looking pretty good. I'm still not sure what kind of finish I will put on this project, maybe I can rip the pages out of the old atlas we have. As I said, Ed always did like maps. I am sitting peacefully with my toast and jam, thinking about this, when there is a knock on the door. I don't answer the door, because I'm a woman alone, and safety is a concern. Whoever it is comes around to the back door. They can clearly see me sitting in my kitchen eating my toast and jam. I can't avoid it, I have to answer the door.

The lady at the door tells me she's the public health nurse, and asks to come in. I tell her she can't. Then she asks me what that terrible smell is. She says that Meals on Wheels called them, concerned that there was something dead in my house. She offers to call a pest control. Now I'm getting really irritated. I'm very seldom rude to people, but this time I do get rude, and tell the woman to go mind her own business, and leave me to mine. When I say it so plainly, she has no choice but to leave.

I go back into the bedroom and complain to Ed about how meddlesome Lillian is. I will definitely cancel Meals on Wheels.

On Sunday morning, I've decided the finish will be maps: maps of family trips we took, mostly in Canada, but a few down south, and one marvelous Caribbean cruise to celebrate our 40th anniversary. I am staring out the front window, at nothing really, when Beatrice pulls up and gets out of the car with a huge bunch of flowers. It hits me then that this is Mother's Day. I sink down on to the couch.

After knocking and calling for a few minutes, Beatrice lets herself in. Of course, she has a key; she's my daughter.

When the smell hits her, she turns white. I can actually see the blood draining away from her face. She goes into the bedroom, and makes a strange noise. I hear her dialing the phone. Then she comes out and sits down beside me on the couch.

One thing I can say for Beatrice, she is always calm. She's well suited to her job as an emergency room nurse.

After a few minutes, I hear the sirens in the background. Then in come the police, fire, and paramedics. Some of them are not so calm.

Beatrice tells me I need to go with her. She is taking me to the hospital. I tell her I want to say good bye to her Dad first. Beatrice agrees.

A few minutes later two firemen come out carrying my project on a stretcher. Ed is kind of sitting up, with his favourite mug in his right hand. His left hand rests on the cufflink box, which is in his lap. His legs are bent, as if he were reading in bed – which he liked to do.

I know this is the last time I'll get to speak to Ed, so I go over to the stretcher and tell him goodbye. I tell him I thought we would be together forever. I apologize that I couldn't make that happen, because when you're old, other people always think they know what is best for you. Of course Ed, being Ed, doesn't answer.

Travel Bonus

I SPOT HER WHILE I'M stowing my suitcase in the plane's overhead compartment. She's wearing a head cover, but no veil. One of the girls caught between the desired "western world" and the old traditions. She'll be an easy one if she's the chosen one. Not much fun in the chase, too timid, but lots of fun in the catch, a virgin if she's not married. These girls marry young, and this one is probably about 19 already, so I look for the toe rings that are the usual wedding gifts from the husband. No toe rings. A virgin. Bonus. I'm not going to get any crotch crickets from her. Another bonus— security. I know this culture. I make it my business to know these things. There has to be three males to swear it's rape, or it's not, and the girl gets it—50 lashes usually, and marked forever, so her marriage chances are gone. They don't complain, these girls. Marriage is even more important to them than it is to Canadian girls. Their laws work for men, and that's the way it should be. So I watch where she's sitting because she's probably the one. She's about eleven rows behind, aisle seat, sitting next to a kid who looks to be about 12 or 13 years old. That's good, an ideal position. I feel a stirring just thinking about it.

The next girl I pick out as she walks past. She's in her early twenties, skinny, no tits, glasses and mousy hair. These plain girls sometimes make the best hits. A good looking man just has to give them one smile, and they don't know what's going on. Their little hearts perk up with the thought that some man has finally found them attractive, they get a little thrill, and their legs fall open. They haven't figured out it isn't love until I'm done.

Pretty slim chance of catching anything from her either.

Maybe her.

But I got to be careful with this type. One took me to court once, charged me with rape. Fortunately the jury figured out that if she was stupid enough to go to a hotel room with a man, she got what was coming to her, and deserved it. Had a good lawyer on that one, I'll admit. I'll use him again if I ever need to. Of course it also worked in my favour that the jury was mostly men.

The ugly duckling, who's past the point of ever turning into a swan, sits down about three seats behind me and one over. Noted. She pulls out a paperback and begins to read. Probably it's one of those romance books—no sex, just lingering looks and heaving hooters.

Now I've got to pick out a third. Those are the rules of the game, and I been playing it a long time. But the third one is never *the* one, just good for my fantasy life. For the third one I always pick a girl I know isn't going to be easy: the professional type, or the outdoorsy type, someone who thinks she's as good as a man any day, and would yell bloody blue murder. Then I just have a few fantasies to enhance the pleasure. Sometimes when I'm doing one, I pretend it's the third pick, and it just adds a little starch.

I pick an outdoorsy type this time, great long brown hair and carrying a backpack that looks stuffed and heavy. I give her one of my best smiles, but she doesn't even give me a second look. That's okay, too muscular anyway. I can see that by her calves. Probably drinks beer and lift weights. She may even be a dyke.

I sit down and do up my seat belt for the take-off. This part used to make me nervous. I read once that approximately 85 percent of accidents happen on takeoff, 13 percent on landing, and the rest in the air. Takeoffs don't bother me as much now though, since I've always got something to look forward to.

As soon as the coffee, tea or me girl comes by I grab a beer. When I get that down, I stand up as if to stretch my legs, and I check things out again. The dyke type is chatting up her neighbour, a man with a kid on his lap. How she thinks she's going to get past the kid is what I'd like to know.

The Mouse is still buried in her book. Anyway, she's one seat in – not the ideal position.

So, my decision is the head scarf girl. She's just sitting there looking a little green. I'd guess that takeoffs don't agree with her. Well, I'll give her something to take her mind off that. I head down to the washroom, hanging my left arm, looking like a farmer. As I pass Scarf Head I move left and grab a handful. Not bad. She's got a little more to squeeze than looked like in that sari, or whatever they call it, but I don't mind those kind of surprises. Scarf Head gives a little screechy gasp and practically climbs on to the kid in the seat next to her. He scowls and give her an elbow, and goes back to his comic book. No help there, Scarf Head.

Felt good.

I like it when they get scared.

On the way back from the washroom I can see the coffee, tea or me girl talking to Scarf Head. I'm not too worried. Those girls don't admit to anything. It does blow my fun on the way back, though.

I sit down and think about The Mouse, but discard that thought almost at once. Her being a seat over is pretty difficult for me, and anyway, she really is as plain as a dog's butt.

Then I think about The Dyke, who's now jiggling the pukey kid on her lap. I think about her for awhile, but then cool it. It's only an hour into a seven hour flight, and I don't want things to go too fast. I ring for the girl and get another beer.

When I hear the server coming down the aisle with the meals I stand up. I stretch like I'm stiff, and I check things out again. I'm pretty good at the timing now, I been doing it for so long. I see one of the servers is a man. I don't know why any self-respecting man would take a job serving people. He doesn't look like a fag. Maybe he's just not smart enough to get a real job.

When the time is right I move down the aisle. Scarf Head is looking down and doesn't see me coming. When I get near the cart I make noises like I'm really sorry, but I got to get to the bathroom no matter what. I murmur what sounds like apologies, and squeeze by on the left side. My timing is perfect. I'm level with the girl when I've got to squeeze by the serving cart, and I shove my crotch right in her hanging-down face. Scarf Head jumps into the next seat. This time the kid doesn't elbow her. He takes a look at me. I give him my best "we're all men of the world" look, but he doesn't seem to be buying it. I see him talking to the man on his right, his father maybe, but the man isn't paying that much attention. He has a bawling kid on the other side, and doesn't appreciate the interruption.

I go relieve myself, and wash up good. I'm picky when it comes to that sort of thing. Don't want to encourage the germs.

On the way back I notice Scarf Head is with the attendant again. She looks even greener than before.

After the movie the lights go down for people to sleep, and I know this is my time. I go back to the washroom, and hang around a bit. The tea or me girls aren't around right now, probably up front doing the pilot.

Just as I hoped, Scarf Head comes down the aisle. She's lurching a bit, which is strange. I'm sure these girls don't drink. Anyway, I don't spend much time wondering about it, because who cares. I grab Scarf Head and shove her into the bathroom. I back her into the sink. She's looking really green now. I get her dress, or whatever it is, up around her hips, get her knickers down, and get in there. It doesn't last too long. I been fantasizing a bit too much, and I get off too quick, but it still feels good. Worth the wait and the planning.

I leave Scarf Head panting against the sink, but I'm hardly out of the bathroom before I hear her vomiting. I can't believe it. Puking over a little slap and tickle like that.

I feel pretty good when I get back to my seat, and so I doze off almost immediately. I don't know what it is about sex that makes you want to sleep, but it does it to me every time.

About an hour or so later I get woke up by the male server. He's going from seat to seat asking everyone if there's a doctor on board. Seems someone got sick. When I look at my watch I can see we're just about an hour out of Toronto, so whoever it is probably isn't going to die before we get there.

Sure enough we land in TO about an hour later, right on time for once. The pilot comes over the intercom and asks everyone to remain seated as they have an ill passenger, and they want to get her off first. Figures. Everyone's tired, and now we got to be delayed by someone getting sick. Some paramedics get on and after a little fuss they come by with someone on a stretcher. Like everyone else I'm interested in seeing who got sick, and I get a little shock when I see it's Scarf Head. Surely she isn't going to claim I made her sick doing her. Looks like I might need that lawyer again. No one stops me, however, and I get through customs, and of course Dorothy is waiting for me. She's a good girl. She'll have something ready for me to eat, and not complain if I don't want to eat it. I give her the perfume I got at the duty free shop.

Dorothy gives me the car keys, and, sure enough, when we get home she's made some of those fancy little pastries for me.

We talk over my trip. Dorothy's always interested in what I see and do on these trips, but of course I don't tell her everything. She's so interested maybe I'll take her with me one day. The company doesn't pay for wives to go, but I don't make bad money, and I probably will take her someday. Maybe.

The next day being Saturday I sleep in late. When I get up Dorothy's blatting at me to listen to the news, so eventually I do. On the news they're talking about a woman who got rushed straight from the airport to the hospital last night. Apparently she's got some kind of disease. They suspect Ebola, and the patient is undergoing testing. In fact, she's in isolation. And on another radio station I hear that everyone who took care of her, including the paramedics, are in isolation. I know right away it's Scarf Head, and now I know why she was looking so green, and puking. It wasn't about the sex at all.

Then they try to reassure the public. They tell the public there is no need to worry, that whatever she has is not communicable by casual contact.

Well, Jesus! What the hell is casual contact? For me the whole thing was casual, but I know damn well the police wouldn't call it casual. What the hell should I do now? Do I go and admit what I did, and get tested? Tell them the girl wanted it? Do I sit tight and wait to turn green and puke?

I decide to sit tight for a few days. I listen to the news all day. Three days later the worst happens. She dies.

The doctor's still don't know what she had. Here I was worried about crotch crickets, and now I probably got some strange, deadly disease. That bitch.

The medical people are still reassuring the public that casual contact with her is not a problem.

But, what about me?

What about my "casual contact"?

Because she's dead.

Dead.

Tips for DIY'ers

I AM A DO-IT-yourselfer. I admit I take on this role with some hesitation. However, in the competition between diminishing money and diminishing time, the money is fast winning the race.

There are some rewards for DIYers. We learn. However reluctantly.

For example, I now know that the pressure of the water running through the little plastic pipe which goes into my furnace humidifier is 34 pounds per square inch. Or maybe that was 64 pounds per square inch. At any rate, it's impossible to staunch the pressure with your hand over the pipe, and the force is enough to drill a hole in your head. For the DIY'er in this situation: don't just stand there trying to staunch the flow, run and turn off the water at the main. With 34 pounds (or 64 pounds) of pressure the basement fills up rapidly. I confess that trying to staunch the flow was a technique I used frequently before I became an experienced DIY'er. For example, when the toilet was overflowing, I would slam down the toilet lid, hoping that would stop the flood. It almost never did.

DIY'ers should always be grateful, and graceful, when receiving information about fixing anything. I got the information about the amount of water pressure in the little plastic pipe when I called for help. "Wow," I thought, "this is really useful if I want to build an indoor pool in my basement."

I did eventually find someone to fix the humidifier, and a few weeks later I was able to turn the water back on. A shower never felt so good. My co-workers were happy for me.

Here's another tip. When you take something apart, look very carefully at the way it comes out. Does the little spring come out first, the round thing second, the wedge-like thing third, and the hook fourth? Or, was it?

If you do forget to look at the order when you take it apart, the correct way to put it back together is the way that seems impossible. If it goes back easy, it can't be right. That would be against the rules.

It took me a few years to figure out the importance of looking at the way everything comes apart. When I removed the inside handle of my screen door the only thing that came out was the handle itself. The springs, washers, screws, lug nuts, retainers, were all attached to the outside handle. So I went outside and carefully noted that the knob came out first, followed by a stick thing, with a spring on it, with the large end toward the inside, and a little round thing. And there I stood, triumphant, knowing it all, outside the closed door, with the handle in my hand.

Books are excellent. Determined not to pay the price of a plumber just to fix my dripping tap, I bought a book. It cost $28.95, but had great pictures. I sat on the toilet lid and looked at the pictures of taps. The picture on page 23 looked quite a lot like my taps, but not quite. The picture on page 48 looked fairly close also, but again not quite. Ditto for the pictures on page 101, 102, and 183.

I drove back to the book store, and talked to the clerk, who was quite knowledgeable. After discussing the fact that the house was quite old, and the plumbing had never been upgraded, I bought another book called "The Antique Plumber's Handbook". At first I was reluctant to purchase it, as it was sealed in plastic and I couldn't really assess the contents, but I finally decided I had to do it. I was not paying a plumber. It cost $42.95.

When I got home I saw that the first picture was of an elderly gentleman, with a satisfied grin on his face, holding up a wrench and various parts of a tap. Briefly, I was concerned that I had purchased a book which featured antique plumbers, rather than antique taps—a kind of elderly fire-fighters calendar, so to speak. I was a little apprehensive about turning the page, fearing there might be a feature on ancient plumber's butts. However, I was soon reassured. Inside the books were beautiful coloured plates featuring those long goose-necked faucets with a tap for cold water only, and wonderful indoor and outdoor pumps.

As none of the pictures were even remotely close to my taps, I referred back to the first book. The pictures on pages 101 and 183 were the closest match, so I proceeded. The insides of the tap were also a fairly close match, and after removing everything I could, I took all of it down to the nearest plumbing store. This is important: find a plumbing store which will look at the insides and match them up with new insides, without making fun of you. I returned with all the insides and installed them. The drip was much reduced. I washed the grease off my hands, wiped as much grease as I could off the books, and drank a glass of wine to celebrate.

Here's another tip: when putting together large furniture ensure you have all the pieces before ripping open the plastic. That way when you go back to the store to convince the clerk that you didn't lose the missing piece, you will be able to demonstrate that the packing material is still intact.

And don't worry if you have a few pieces left over when you build that bookcase, as long as the furniture holds together. The extra parts are there to make up for the important piece that wasn't packed in the first place.

Another important tip: build the large furniture in the room in which it will remain. That way you won't have to take it apart again in order to get it into that room.

One more tip: send your children over to the neighbours before you start any project. Yes, they will say "Mommy told me I had to stay over here for breakfast, lunch and supper because she's changing the door knob." But think how much more preferable that is than for them to go over the next day and say "Mommy said #%***$@&&**" when she was changing the door knob yesterday."

Magnet this article to your fridge, and happy DIY'ing.

Rescue

I'M SITTING ON MY BED crying softly when Robin walks in, doesn't knock or anything, just walks in like it's her room. It used to be her room too, and she's the one who moved out, but it's like she still thinks it's her room.

"What's the matter, Krissy," she says.

I have no idea how she knows I'm in trouble. Mom and Dad's bedroom is right next to mine, and Robin's room is way across on the other side of the front room, so I know she didn't hear me, because if I had been making noise Mom would have been in here.

Robin and I are identical twins, in looks that is, but not in any other way. It was great when we were kids because we fooled our friends and cousins and teachers. We couldn't fool Mom and Dad, though; somehow they always knew who was who. It got to be a drag when we were older, because we really are so different. Robin, who is named after a cute little bird, is hard as a rock, and me, Krystal, named after a rock, is as soft as, well, a cute little bird. I think somehow our parents messed up our names.

That's not the only difference between us either. Robin is a whizz in chemistry, math and physics. She's so good at chemistry that she tutors Rocco, the school football quarter back, who is in grade 11, a whole grade ahead of us. And me, I love books and poetry, particularly Wordsworth, and when I read *Gone With the Wind* I longed to be Scarlett. Of course, I was only 12 then, and now I'm 15 and know better. And I make my spending money babysitting the neighbours "rotten brats", as Robin calls them.

When I got tired of being mistaken for my sister, I cut my hair, not too short, just to shoulder length, but Robin left her hair long, and now everyone can tell us apart.

But I guess that's how Robin knew I was crying, because we are still twins, despite our differences.

So I tell her. I trust my sister; I know she won't judge me, and I know she won't tell Mom or Dad.

I tell her how bad I messed up. I tell her how I went to the party at Kevin's place. It was an awesome party, at first. Kevin's parents are visiting his older sister in Calgary, waiting for their first grandchild, then the dad is returning to Toronto and the mom is staying to help for a few weeks. So of course it was a great party, with lots of beer and wine, and some other drinks, and the smell tells me that people have been smoking up. I don't really drink booze, so I was only drinking punch that someone had made.

"Dufus, don't you know what people do to punch?" Robin asks me. Well, I guess I kind of did, but I ignored it.

Anyway, I've had a terrible crush on Kevin since grade 7, and he is kind of popular, being the point guard on the basketball team. So when he asked me to come into his parents room and see his basketball trophies, I hesitated only a little. And Jessie, who used to bully me back in grade school, and always brags that Kevin likes her, was at the party, so I thought I would get one up on her and go with him.

Big, big mistake.

We sat on the bed and French kissed and cuddled a bit, and then Kevin got pushy, and started trying to feel my breasts. Well, I guess I let him, a bit.

"Nothing wrong with that. That's perfectly normal," my sister says, and I feel a little better.

But then he said to me to show him my titties.

"What? He said 'titties'? Jaysus, you're not an eff-ing cow," Robin hisses.

Only she doesn't say "eff-ing" but the real thing.

Then she just looks at me, and I have to say it. I did it. And even worse. Kevin had been fooling around with his cell phone, and when I flashed him—and it was just for a second—he took a picture.

Now I really start to wail. We hear stirring in Mom and Dad's room, and Robin calls out to let them know I just have a bad stomach and she has already made me a tea and a hot water bottle, and will stay with me till I feel better.

But now I have to tell her the worst part. Kevin says he is going to post that picture on Facebook unless I give him a BJ. And I have one week, till next Friday evening, to tell him which it will be.

"What the fuck?" says Robin, puts her arm around me, and pulls my head to her shoulder. Somehow I feel better. We stay that way for a few minutes. Then she props up the pillows, pushes me back against them and tells me I better go to sleep. She'll try and figure a way out of this for me. Just as she goes out the door she does the strangest thing. She takes a picture of me with her cell phone. What the hell was that about?

I feel better for having told someone. Let's face it, I feel better for having told my sister. She is the least judgemental person I know. When someone at school tries a different fashion, and other people make fun, Robin will compliment that person on their clothes. And when Rocco came out as being gay she didn't give it any thought. Actually, it seemed like no one did, but when I mentioned this to Robin she told me I was just stupid, because Rocco is six feet tall, and 90 kilos, and the football hero, so who the hell is going to say anything to him?

The next day is Sunday, and I mope around the house and tell Mom my stomach is still bothering me, so I don't go out. After that is Monday, and I tell Mom my stomach still hurts and spend the day in bed. Tuesday I do the same thing, and both Mom and Dad are seriously worried because I don't generally miss school.

The truth is, my stomach is really upset. I feel like vomiting whenever I think about putting Kevin's thing in my mouth. But what choice do I have?

On Wednesday morning, Robin comes into my room, and I gape at her. She's cut her hair off, cut it off as short as mine. I barely register what she's saying, I'm so dumbfounded. Eventually I figure out that she's telling me to get up and go to school, that I can't stay home the rest of my life. I'll have to go back and it might as well be today. Also, our parents are probably going to call an ambulance for me if I stay home another day. Somehow I get through the day. I avoid Kevin as much as possible, and when I see him smirking at me, I go red, I put my head down, and walk off as fast as I can.

Thursday morning, I'm dragging my feet getting ready for school, dreading another day, when Robin walks into my room again without knocking. I really don't care. I only have today and tomorrow left before I have to blow Kevin.

"Check your email" says Robin.

"What?"

"Just do it."

So I do. And there is an email from Robin, no text, just an attachment. I open the attachment, and for a few seconds I don't know what I'm seeing, then it registers. There is a clear picture of Kevin on some bed, shirt on but no pants, and there is Rocco, one huge arm wrapped around Kevin's shoulders. Rocco is grinning at Kevin with affection. Kevin's face is a mixture of surprise and horror. But no one is going to notice his expression. All they are going to see is Kevin in bed with gay Rocco.

Now I know why Robin took my picture. To have a picture for when she cut her hair to look like me.

"Kevin thought you were me," I say.

"Yup. He really thought he was going to get lucky. He almost came when I told him to get on the bed and drop his pants. He wasn't so excited when Rocco came in, though. I had my cell phone ready, and there you go. Your blackmail material is better than what he's got."

I feel a big smile starting.

"Tell Kevin to suck his own dick" says Robin, "and you owe me $50.00 for the haircut, but I can wait for it."

As writers, we normally try to avoid clichés. The following short story contains 56 clichés, in 650 words. With a few more in the rejection letter.

The Cliché

I HAD THOUGHT THAT THE job would go smoother.

We had come full circle in our planning, and like kids in a candy store we thought we would clear the place out lock, stock and barrel. But it turned out that the long arm of the law had been tipped off. They had left no stone unturned, and decided to nip it in the bud.

This is how it all went down.

I had suggested that the fact of the matter was that the best time to close the deal would be near the end of banking hours, and when all was said and done, the rest of the gang agreed with me. Billy felt that lunch time, with some of the employees out of the building, was a better time, but in the current climate, the gang didn't care, in any way, shape or form, how many employees were present. This was my first big heist, my baptism by fire, and I was glad Billy's suggestions fell on deaf ears. Every dog has his day, and today was my chance to shine. Up till now I had been too shy to make suggestions, but by hook and by crook, I gained some confidence in my planning abilities, and got behind the eight ball. Billy cursed a bit, but everyone knew he had a checkered career, and his successes were few and far between. Although there was never a dull moment when Billy was around, the winds of change were here, and everyone looked to me for the strategy.

At this moment in time, the gang consisted of people from all walks of life, and if these walls could talk, they would tell a tale with never a dull moment.

Jake was a good one for thinking outside the box, but others pointed out it wasn't a level playing field, and he was seeing only the tip of the iceberg. Jake was thick as thieves with Ben, the leader, however, at the end of the day, he decided to leave the group. The rest of the gang decided they were in, hook, line and sinker.

In the final analysis, we decided to take the path of least resistance, take the tiger by the tail, and go in with guns a-blazing. I was posted just outside the door to deter any cops who might get the bright idea to storm the building. But it turned out that the police had been thinking outside the box. To give the devil his due, they, with the patience of Job, had been hiding out in the building all day, and were now chomping at the bit, just waiting for us.

When the action began there was a mass exodus of the clients closest to the door. That was par for the course, so I just let them go. For a few minutes all was quiet, but I suspected it was the calm before the storm, and suddenly all hell broke loose. The police opened fire, and several of the gang bit the dust, including Ben, who was shot dead as a doornail. I quickly saw that to all intents and purposes the heist was over, and figured I would not stick around to the bitter end.

I decided to make good my escape, and walked away just in the nick of time.

The rest of the gang went to trial, and are now paying the piper. I am sure the sands of time are moving very slowly for them.

Well, the fact of the matter is that in this day and age bank robbers do not get a fair shake. However, it's no use crying over spilt milk, and when all was said and done, I saw the writing on the wall. I decided to go into a different line of work and become a writer. I have received my first rejection letter, copied below. It cut me to the quick. However, patience is a virtue, and it is my intention to try, and try again.

Dear Sir

The story you submitted was reviewed by several people, and I was nominated to take the hit for the team and write this letter. It is generally a task that I avoid like the plague; however, it is all in a day's work.

I regret to inform you that your submission does not fit the bill at this point in time.

I hate to burst your bubble, and I don't like to step on anyone's toes, however, crime stories are a dime a dozen, and as you know, when it rains it pours, and we have been flooded with similar submissions.

For what it's worth, being older and wiser, I include a brief critique of your story.

It goes without saying that in this day and age correct spelling and grammar are necessary, and in this regard your document is letter perfect.

Unfortunately you lack the capacity to think outside the box, and so your submission is simply the same old story, as dull as dishwater. Some of us who read your story were bored to tears. I know that sounds harsh, but I need to call a spade, a spade. It would not be of benefit for me to gild the lily.

If you think there is a light at the end of the tunnel for this story, you are sadly mistaken, for there is not a hope in hell.

It is certainly not the end of the world to have a manuscript rejected, and I urge you to leave no stone unturned in putting your best foot forward.

It is important for you to know the ropes, so please keep a stiff upper lip, put your nose to the grindstone, your shoulder to the wheel, start from scratch, and you may yet find a good fit. You simply need to go back to the drawing board.

Bear in mind that you are a new author, and still wet behind the ears. Writing is a tough row to hoe, but please don't think that you are in over your head, or that you have bitten off more than you can chew. It really is not a wild goose chase.

Go for broke, write till the cows come home, and you will have your fifteen minutes of fame.

Sincerely,
S. Joseph
Publisher

Up on the Roof

THEY'RE NUTS, BOTH OF THEM. Well, not too bad yet, just one brick short of a load, one card short of a deck. One has Alzheimer, one has dementia, which is which I don't remember, but what does it matter. They're both a few sandwiches short of a picnic.

But what the hell, they are my parents.

My sister, Melanie, takes care of them, but when it comes to the manly stuff, that's my job. Winter's coming on, and I'm checking the big items, the things a man should do. And I'm the son, so it's my job. But first I'll take mom and dad out for breakfast.

I listen to the oldies for the entire drive up. I've got them all on CD's, and I really like The Drifters. Some of the songs I listen to twice, especially the one "Up On The Roof". It's an hour drive, and sometimes I stress about how I will find the parents are doing, but the oldies keep me mellow.

It's not too bad when I get there. They're delighted to see me, and even more so when I say I'll take them out to breakfast. Mom's in her old green bathrobe, and she insists she can go to breakfast in that, because now she's old, and doesn't have to look good for anyone.

"You can't go to breakfast in your bathrobe" I say.

"Why not?"

"Green isn't your best colour." I tell her.

I look in her wardrobe, pull out a blue sweater and hold it up to her chin.

"Look Ma. Look at how blue your eyes are with this sweater."

She chases me out of the room so she can change, and when she comes out I tell her again how the sweater brings out the blue in her eyes.

Breakfast isn't too bad, either. Dad insists on telling century-old jokes to the busy waitress, and mom changes her mind three times about what she wants to eat. First she wants pancakes, then bacon and eggs, then pancakes again, but only if they have "real" maple syrup. I tip the waitress double for her patience. I get them into the car with a minimum of bickering about who gets to ride shotgun. Dad insists he should be in the front because he's "The Man", and mom advises him that it's not 1950 anymore and "The Man" doesn't get to do everything he wants to do. Mom wins this battle because Dad moves away from the car, waving his arms around to make a point, and Mom simply opens the front door and gets in. Dad sighs, gives up, and gets into the back, and we're away. We are almost home again when Dad asks me to check on the roof shingles. He found one in the back yard and saved it. I assure him I'll check it out.

When we get back Mom and Dad thank me for breakfast. I go in search of a ladder, find some roofing nails, and get up on the roof. I don't like heights, and this is two storeys. The back section over the kitchen is a flat roof. I cross the roof in a crouch, and, of course, the missing shingle is up on the pitched roof part. I creep slowly and cautiously up the pitch and replace the shingle. I'm just hammering roofing nails into some of the other loose shingles, when I hear Dad.

"Call the police, Marie," he hollers. "There's a burglar on the roof. He's trying to get in the house."

"What?" Mom calls back. She's going deaf, but will never admit it. For once I'm glad. It will buy me some time while Dad tries to make her understand, or finally gives up and goes to call 911 himself.

I inch carefully over the down slope of the pitched roof to the front of the house, where I know a window will be open, and yell for my dad. He's still roaring at Mom to call the police when he recognizes something, my voice maybe, and comes out on to the lawn.

"Tom," he says. "How nice to see you. When did you get here? Marie, come on out, it's Tom. Why are you up on the roof, Tom?"

Mom comes out and gazes up at me with astonishment. "What are you doing up there, Tom?"

They invite me to come in and have some breakfast with them. It takes a while to convince them that I was here earlier and took them out to breakfast. Melly says they forget to eat. Now I believe her. It takes another few minutes to explain why I'm up on the roof. Eventually I promise I'll come in and have some breakfast with them when I'm done. It doesn't matter. They won't remember my promise in ten minutes anyway.

"Be careful up there, it's pretty steep," Dad calls as they go back into the house.

About twenty minutes later, I'm done, and I crawl cautiously back over the pitched roof to the flat section. The ladder is gone. I reluctantly clamber back over the pitched roof and yell for Dad over the open window. The TV's on loud, so I know Mom's watching her soap. After a few minutes of me yelling and banging on the roof, Dad comes out again. He regards me with aggravation and asks me what I want this time. "Dad, where's the ladder?" I ask.

"Your mom told me to lock it in the garage so burglars can't get up on the roof," he says, and goes back into the house.

So I start yelling for him again.

Dad comes back out and tells me to stop yelling and not be so rude. He also informs me that I'll have to wait, they're watching a show, but he'll get the ladder when the show's over.

I holler a bit, but it's no use.

I inch back over the pitched roof to the flat part, and pull out my cell phone. I dial my sister's cell. There's no answer. She takes care of the parents all the time and works part time nearby so she can go home and make their lunch, or be there in an emergency. Now she's finally got a few hours to herself, and she probably figures whoever's calling her will just have to wait. I wonder briefly if she's checked the caller ID and decided that I should deal with whatever the problem is by myself. I leave a message on her voice mail, but don't hold out much hope.

I settle down on the flat roof area waiting for the soap to end. I hope it's a half-hour show, and not an hour one. It's pretty hot up here even though we're now into September. I wait. And wait. The old Drifters song, about being up on the roof, where all your cares just drift into space comes back to me. I sing it softly. My version includes a lot of humming, although I do remember the one line about getting away from the hustling crowds. I could use a little crowd right now, I think.

I check my watch. Near the half hour time I scramble back over the pitched roof. I notice that I don't mind it so much, and I remind myself not to get careless. Over the front window I bellow for my dad again. He comes out, reassuring me that he didn't forget me. I crawl back over the pitched roof for the umpteenth time, holler at my dad who's carrying the ladder to the front of the house, and finally convince him I should get down from the flat roof side.

We're just finishing breakfast again when Melly walks in.

"How'd it go?" she asks.

"Had some breakfast, fixed the roof, had some breakfast." I say. Melly looks like she wants to tell me I'm repeating myself, but then apparently thinks better of it. I get ready to go.

I'm back in the car, singing to The Drifters again. This time it's "You've got your troubles, I've got mine". Then it's "Under The Boardwalk. I hesitate for a minute, and decide I'm being paranoid. I don't know of any boardwalks, and anyway, I'm not really superstitious. But just in case, I'll stay away from the beach for the next few weeks.

Gumdrop Tree

MY YOUNGEST SISTER'S FIRST MEMORY is of being carried down the gravel road by my oldest sister. Can an adult really remember what happened before they were even old enough to walk? I doubted it, but she brought up the memory, not me. And I do remember it.

My father, in a rage, roared at all of us to "get out, get out and don't come back". My mother, whose main role in life besides cooking, cleaning, and endless laundry, was placating my father, shooed us out the door.

So there we were, four little girls in charity box dresses, and one baby in a cloth diaper, escaping, headed for the hills. There were no hills, so we hiked up the path everyone called "The Old Vault Road". This dirt path was so named because about a mile up from the main road, the gravel road, was an old structure built into the side of a hill. It had been used years ago to house the bodies of people who died in the winter. They remained there until the ground thawed enough to bury them in the spring.

About a mile up The Old Vault Road we simply left the path and walked into the woods. It was spring. This I know because the lilacs were in bloom, and they were glorious, so that even in our flight we noticed their beauty.

The next question, for my sister and me, was how to entertain the three younger kids. Judging from the fact that my youngest sister needed to be carried, I must have been about ten years old. So my oldest sister would have been eleven, and the younger ones one, three, and five.

What did we do during that long day? Who really knows how long it was? It seemed very long from a ten-year olds point of view. In the afternoon I snuck home and got food and something to drink. And I got gumdrops. Candy was a rare treat.

When I returned to the woods, my older sister and I had a conference. She distracted our little sisters while I stuck the gumdrops on the twigs of nearby bushes. We then told our sisters of the existence of a rare and wonderful tree that grew gumdrops. We said we had heard that one grew in this area, and told the little girls to go and look. To their wonder and delight they found the tree, and a feast of candy.

I have no idea what time we returned home, or what my father's mood was when we did.

Many, many years later this story was told to children and grandchildren, but differently. It became a story of the rare, elusive gum drop tree, of the children's delight in finding candy— candy deep in the forest. Oh, the mystery and joy of it then.

How I Became a High School Drop-out

I BECAME A HIGH SCHOOL dropout last night. My Mom doesn't know it yet, but that's the way it is. It was because of Grandma, not that I'm blaming her, or anything. She was the one who always told me I had to get an education, and if she could understand what went on she would be pretty upset. Of course, if she could understand, it wouldn't have happened.

Grandma's a little girl. That's how my mother puts it. I say she's a couple fries short of a happy meal. But I can remember when Grandma used to crawl under the weeping willow into my fort and play cowboys with me. And I can remember when I broke Mom's antique soup tureen, and Grandma told Mom she did it, said her fingers were getting clumsy in her old age. So, if Grandma ever breaks anything, I'll cover for her. Know what I mean?

It was Friday night, grocery night, and I was taking care of Grandma 'till Mom got home, which I was praying was going to happen real soon. 'Cause, baby, tonight was the night. I got a date with Julia. Julia, not Julie—she's real strong on that. Julia, of the long blonde hair and the big brown eyes, and the—whew—body.

How'd I do that? You might well ask.

Hey, I'm cool. And it doesn't hurt that I play basketball. I'm not that tall, and I'm pretty skinny. My friends call me "Knobs", short for "Knobbly Knees", but I can live with the shortened version. What gets me noticed is that I sure can jump, and that night I made the winning basket, so I was feeling pretty hot.

Also, I had just about perfected my saunter.

Right after the game I sauntered up to Julia and asked her out. I thought all my bodily fluids had dried up the way my tongue stuck to the roof of my mouth. I think I sort of stuttered at first, but I guess she didn't notice, because she said "yes". Hey, I was cool. And before I could explain how my car was in the garage (r-i-i-ght) she offered to pick me up—in her little red Fiero, no less. A two seater.

Only thing that was supposed to happen was for Mom to come home on time.

I'd even got it figured out what I was gonna say when the guys asked me if I got to first base, or anywhere at all. I didn't want them to think I was a wimp, or a wussy, or something, but I didn't want them to think that Julia was easy, either. What if that got back to her? There sure as hell wouldn't be a second date. So, I was just gonna smile and tell them they had to ask the lady if they were that interested. That would save both her, and my cool.

Only my big problem now was where the heck was Mom? Sometimes she has trouble with the old Buick when it gets cold, and it was definitely cold tonight. I sure hoped car problems wasn't the case, because it was only about a half hour till Julia would be showing up.

I guess I should have told Mom I had a date with my dream girl, and endured the teasing. At least then I would have known she'd make an extra effort to get home on time. Instead, I just told her I was going out. Now she didn't know how important this was to me.

So, I had to get into the shower.

Grandma was in the living room looking at pictures in some old magazine. She was in a blue dress with little pink flowers, and her white hair was kind of standing up in the back. She always remembers to comb her hair in the front, but she forgets the back. Mom says that's because she can't see the back. I got a comb and tried to smooth down the back of her hair, but she pushed my hand away.

I can remember when Grandma used to dress pretty sharp for an old lady, but these days Mom puts her in those dresses with the velcro down the back. She says it makes things a lot easier when she gets Grandma dressed in the morning.

Edgy People

I got Grandma settled in front of the T.V. She just loves that show "Friends". I locked the front door, and the back door, and used the hook and eye on the back door where it's put up high so Grandma can't reach it when Mom's not in the same room. I put the deadbolt on the front door.

Then I got into the bathroom and started to get changed. I knew laundry day was coming up, because the only clean towels were those old paisley ones that always get used last. No matter, I got a new shampoo. It's supposed to make my hair soft, in case Julia wants to run her hands through it, ya know.

The whole time I was getting changed I kept talking to Grandma. I took off my jeans and called out, "How's the show, Grandma?"

I needed her to answer me so that I knew where she was.

"Why are you yelling?" she hollered back.

I took off my underwear and called out, "What are they doing now, Grandma?"

"Just talking," she replied.

Then I jumped under the water and lathered up and washed my hair real fast. Soon as I turned off the water I called out to Grandma again and asked her if the show was good.

No answer.

I had a problem.

I shot out of the shower so fast I skidded all over the tiles. I grabbed that damned paisley towel off the rack, wrapped it around my waist, and hustled out into the hall. I knew I'd better check the doors first, and, sure enough, the front door was open. There was my Grandma down at the end of the drive, in her fluffy bedroom slippers and bare legs, and shit, it was freezing out there.

I zipped out the door holding that bloody little towel around my waist, still so hot from the shower that clouds of steam billowed up from off me. For a second there I thought a fog had come up. Thank God, we lived out of town so there wasn't any neighbours to see this performance.

I grabbed Grandma by the hand, but she swatted me away. No way she was coming back in. Now, what are you going to do with an 89 year old woman who isn't cooperating? You sure aren't going to pull her around. So, I figure I had to pick her up and carry her back.

Believe me, you don't know how difficult it is to pick up somebody and hold a towel around your waist at the same time, especially when that somebody doesn't want to be picked up, and you're standing on ice. Grandma only weighs about 90 lbs., but she was fighting, and I was sliding around, my bare feet freezing, and trying to hold that paisley towel in place.

I had just got Grandma off the ground when the towel went. Then I heard a car. It was some old beater on its last couple of miles. I had a second of wild hope that it was my Mom, and she would take charge. But it was an old station wagon I had never seen before that pulled up.

Out jumped a youngish woman and this large older woman dressed in a fluffy pink jacket, carrying a big black purse. I don't know what they thought I was doing to the old lady, but they flew to the rescue, and practically pulled her out of my arms, which wasn't too hard because I was scrambling around trying to get that towel over my family jewels. They hustled the old lady into their car pretty dammed fast. At that point I tried an explanation.

"But it's my Grandma." I yelled after them. That got me some action.

"Oh my god, that's even worse" the humongous pink woman screeched, then turned and came after me. That was the last thing I heard for a while. Those plastic purses get real hard in the cold.

I was just surfacing when I heard the sound of a well-tuned engine. The station wagon was gone. I was bare assed in the snow bank with something running down my face. There was blood in the snow beside me, and that paisley towel was nowhere to be seen.

The red Fiero pulled up. I didn't even try to think what I was going to say. I just threw some snow over my parts, which were pretty shrunken anyway, and stayed where I was. The Fiero left real quick.

Go back to school tomorrow? I don't think so.

Unravelling

THEY THINK I'M DOTTY, I know they do. Only now they call it Alzheimer's, or Dementia. Fancy words for plain talking, although I think it is better saying it the proper way. Before, the words were insulting, now they're scientific. "Early onset dementia," I heard the doctor diagnose Mrs. Wilson across the hall. "Early onset," the nurse snorted after the doctor left, "the woman's 74." That gave me a chuckle. It sounded "early" to me, but I guess not to the nurse who is all of 30 or so.

Pink is the first colour in my scarf. Pink is for Lizzy. Lizzy left us when she was three, and I was five. One minute we were playing in the small front yard. Then I went in and got a drink of water, and when I came out she was gone. First my mother went up and down the street, saying she couldn't have gone far, she was only three. I was on the swing, pretending I was flying, so I didn't pay much attention. Then suddenly there were people all over the place, men mostly, and they were looking through the house, in the coal cellar, the ice box, the room that Lizzy and I shared, looking in the closets, and then going down the street knocking on people's doors. Even my nine year old brother Jake was looking through the house. And Mrs. Rigollo was making tea for everyone, and giving me peanut butter cookies. Nobody found Lizzy, not to this day.

There are three rows for Lizzy, because she was only three years old.

Next I chose red and black, one of those fancy yarns with the colours mixed together. Red for anger, and black for sadness, because that's how everything felt for a while after Lizzy disappeared. Two rows only. Even though it felt like it lasted forever, I do not want to give it a lot of attention.

Pale green is next, a happy time. I went to the prom, and my dress was pale green. Donny asked me, not Jerome, the football player I longed after, but Donny, who belonged to the chess club and was a little pimply. And he was nice, a gentleman, bringing me a wrist corsage as was the fashion and opening doors for me. I wonder what happened to him? A nice, plain boy. He deserved a good wife and children to love. I wish I had kept in touch with him, but it's too late now. Donny, I hope life was good to you.

"Who's that scarf for, Marta?" The Sergeant asks. She's not really a sergeant, but that's what I call her. She bosses me around, and I do what she says, because when she talks to me she looks at me, and when I talk to her, she listens. She knows I'm still a person, despite my age, and how I look. Her real name is Penny.

"Are you giving that to your great granddaughter? The colours are amazing. It'll sure keep somebody warm." I tell Penny that the scarf is for me.

"Well, it's cold out today, so a warm scarf will help," Penny replies, ignoring the fact that I don't go outside anymore.

Actually, I hardly go out of my room anymore. It's just too much of an effort. Okay, that's one of the reasons I'm fond of Penny. She sees the positive, and doesn't hasten to tell me I'm wrong, or that I don't make sense.

A bright yellow strip is next. The yellow is for my teaching days. I loved being independent, even though I had to board with a local family. I loved being able to open up those children's minds, take them to different places and times in their imagination. They had little else. I like to think they loved me a little, too. Of course, I wasn't allowed to teach after I got married; those were the County rules then. Married women were not hired; they were supposed to be at home taking care of their husbands. So the bright yellow part is also three rows, one for each year I taught.

White is the next colour, and it has a lot of rows. White, because I wore white when I got married. That was only one day, but the marriage lasted. There is one thin black stripe about a quarter ways through the white. That was when I had an affair. It only lasted six or seven months, and Joe never found out, thank God. After it ended, I couldn't believe I risked my family for sex. Because that was what it was, just sex. No one looking at me today could probably even imagine there was a time when I enjoyed sex, but, yes, even the very old used to have sex. It's only natural, you know.

"How're you doing, Marta?" asks The Sergeant. That's another thing I like about Penny. She calls me Marta, not Martha. When I first came to live here, I corrected the staff constantly, not in a mean way, but I wanted to be called by my own name. Finally I had had enough, and decided to refuse to answer to Martha. I did this for about a week, but then I heard a nurse (not The Sergeant) tell the doctor that I was deteriorating rapidly, that I wouldn't even answer to my own name anymore. The doctor told the nurse to let me call myself by whatever name I wanted.

After I overheard that conversation I decided to just answer to Martha. I must say that the staff all seemed delighted that my memory had made such a miraculous recovery.

Brown is my next colour, for my oldest child, Diane. Joe and I named her Diana, but in her early teens she insisted on being called Diane, complaining that Diana was just too dramatic. I guess most people would pick a more feminine colour for a girl, but brown suits Diane. She was always a serious, closed off little girl, who grew into a serious, closed off woman. Diane never married, and her work as a lawyer seems to be her only interest. She's at an age when she can consider retiring, but then what would she do with her time? I always wondered if I could have done a better job with Diane, whether I failed her somehow.

Blue is for Joe junior; we called him JJ for short. He came along when Diane was two. A chubby, happy boy, with big blue eyes, he became a kind, conscientious man, who married a kind woman. He coached his son's baseball team and his daughter's ringette, and brought my two grandchildren to visit me every last Saturday of the month.

These rows here are pretty, lilac and pale purple. Purple was always Clarisse's favourite colour. My youngest, born when JJ was four and Diane almost seven, Clarisse was energetic, rebellious, but always kind. She was the girl who defended the unpopular children in middle school, who auditioned for every star performance in school plays, and who snuck out her window late at night to hang out with friends. She lives in Ireland now with her 20 year old daughter, whom I have only seen twice, and no husband.

"Look at the sun" Penny says, pulling the drapes. "It's nice and warm now. You won't need that scarf till next winter. Just look at it. If it gets much longer you're going to be able to wrap it around yourself several times. You won't even need a coat next winter."

"Penny" I say. "I want this to go with me."

"Go where with you?"

"Into my coffin," I say."

I can see that Penny wants to tell me I won't get cold once I'm in there, but she refrains. She isn't insensitive. So I say it myself, make it into a joke, and Penny laughs. But then I tell her I'm serious, that this scarf has meaning for me, and she says she'll tell the family that's what I want. I tell her thank you, and I mean it. I can't explain to Penny why this scarf is important, I don't even want to explain, but it is important to me.

After the purple come a couple rows of sparkly yarn, blues, and greens and pinks. Joe and I went on a cruise after the kids grew up. It wasn't the first time we had travelled together, but it was special. We renewed our vows. We thought about them, and talked about them, and wrote the vows. We vowed to be more appreciative, to talk more, and to remember why we valued each other. It did bring us closer. When Joe retired, we both worked to be more considerate.

These black rows are for when Joe died, of heart failure at only 67. It was a time of sorrow for me. I was angry for a little while too, that Joe had been taken from me when he was so young. But mostly, I was sad.

I remind Penny frequently now that I want this scarf to be buried with me. I also tell JJ, who looks puzzled and asks why. I can`t explain, I tell him, but that`s what I want. JJ says he will make sure it`s done. He tells me my granddaughter, Heather, will be married this fall, and she wants me to attend. JJ says he will pick me up and bring me back whenever I want, but I tell him I`m just too tired now. I wish the young couple all the best, and call Diane and ask her to give them a cheque for $100.00 from my account.

When I was thinking about power of attorney, Diane pointed out, quite correctly, that it was about the law, not about being nice, and she was a lawyer, and JJ was a plumber.

Tomorrow I will start on grey. The grey is for Lizzy again. Lizzy as a grey ghost. She is coming back to me now, after 82 years, coming during that time between wakefulness and sleep. She is still three years old, but somehow mature, and she tells me that it`s okay, that I'll find only rest and peace. She says that I'll be with her again, and with Joe again. I`m so tired now, and life isn`t that good to me. I`m ready.

***

"There`s really nothing of any value here, Pammy," says Diane, surveying the room.

"Penny," says Penny.

"Clarisse is flying in, so the funeral will be on Friday. I know Mom was fond of you, so if there is anything you want here, help yourself. The rest can go to charity."

Penny crosses the room and picks up the long scarf off the bed. "Your mom wanted this to be buried with her," she says.

"Penny`s right," JJ says. "Mom told me that several times."

"I`m not putting that ugly thing in with her," says Diane. "Look at it. There`s no pattern to it, none of the colours complement each other and it's all grimy from being dragged on the floor. Look at the last rows. The ends haven`t even been finished, they`re all unravelling."

"I can tidy up the ends," offers Penny.

"She really wanted it to go with her," says JJ.

"Forget it," says Diane.

"Diane, I know you have the power of attorney and all, but Mom asked me a couple times for this to go with her. Obviously it meant something to her."

"We can put it by her feet and no one will see it," says Penny.

"Forget it," says Diane again.

She takes the scarf from Penny and drops it in the trash basket. Penny thinks for a moment of retrieving it, but really, what would she do with it? At six o'clock, the scarf is carried out with the rest of the garbage.

The Fridge and the Calendar

FEBRUARY 14

On the fridge: a newspaper blueprint for a house, with "den" written over the "fourth bedroom" designation, held in place by flower and dinosaur magnets; a "Better Half" joke: "Stanley and I settle all our differences like two rational screaming idiots", held in place by a magnet advertising breakfast food; a crayon picture of a blue sky, huge flowers and three stick figures done in bright, primary colours, signed by Tiffany and held in place by a happy face magnet; a grocery list and menus for the week, held in place by a Mickey Mouse magnet.

On the calendar: Call sitter, meet J 6pm Rocco's Pasta Palace yum, yum.

FEBRUARY 26

On the fridge: the house blueprint; the "Better Half" joke; a second crayon drawing of a cheerful dragon done in blues and reds, signed by Tiffany, and held in place by a lady bug magnet and a butterfly magnet purchased for this specific purpose; a new menu and a grocery list.

On the calendar: J. working late. AGAIN the housework is all mine, again.

MARCH 18

On the fridge: the blueprint; the "Better Half" cartoon; an article cut from a magazine— "Why we can't communicate. According to recent studies, men interrupt women five times more often than women interrupt men. Men think they're smarter than they actually are, while women tend to underestimate their own intelligence. Often, men don't seem to be listening because they're not hearing; men suffer hearing loss earlier in life and at twice the rate women do"— the menu and a grocery list.

On the calendar: 7 p.m. marriage counselor, 451 Oak St.

APRIL 14

On the fridge: the blueprint; the article – "Why we can't communicate", a crayon drawing of a flower garden signed by Tiffany, this year's school picture of a six year old girl, the grocery list.

On the calendar: Confirm with sitter. M's party 8 p.m.

JUNE 4

On the fridge: the magazine article; a Maxine joke: "You know what leprechauns and men have in common? Most things you tell them go right over their heads"; a crayon drawing of three stick people and a house done in blues and greens, the school picture, the menu and a grocery list.

On the calendar: Counselor 7 p.m.

AUGUST 3

On the fridge: A Maxine joke: "There is nothing like an extended cruise! Why don't you take one? Leave today."; a partial grocery list held in place by a magnet featuring a mouse and a piece of cheese with the inscription: "Age is not important unless you are a cheese", the school picture, a grocery list.

On the calendar: J. picking up his junk (don't forget dirty clothes), coffee with Mary 7 p.m.

SEPTEMBER 12

On the fridge: a child's picture with two large stick people and one very small stick person, with a storm in the background, done in dark blue and black and signed by Tiffany, the school picture, a grocery list.

On the calendar: Lawyer 3p.m. 1242 Lawrence Ave.

DECEMBER 18

On the fridge: the program from a school Christmas Concert, the child's picture with two large stick people and one very small stick person, with a storm in the background, done in dark blue and black and signed by Tiffany, a grocery list.

On the calendar: Lawyer apt. 3 p,m. Dental apt. for T. 6 p.m.

JANUARY 23

On the fridge: two Maxine cartoons: (1) "If you insist on dating younger men expect some immaturity – just like dating older men", (2) "Why don't they have re-cycling centers where you could drop off your ex-husband?"

On the calendar: J. picking up T. 6 p.m. for the weekend. Drinks M & G 6p.m.

No Fighting

IT'S ALMOST MIDNIGHT WHEN WE GET to the last call on our work sheet, and I say to Vern that I think maybe this customer might be a little sore, so let me do the talking. Vern's a nice guy, most of the time, but he isn't what you would call diplomatic. The customer's appointment was between two and five in the afternoon, and so we're six hours late, and I wouldn't blame them for being pissed off.

The woman who answers the door is good looking, long blonde hair and a great body, but she's taller than Vern. Vern tends to not like that in a woman. He likes women to look up to him, both physically and in every other way.

Me, I'm a little over six foot, and stocky, but Vern is short and kind of skinny, and he's always out to prove himself. It can get tiresome.

I apologize immediately to the lady for being so late, and tell her that we had a lot of trouble at the last place, had to remove all the doors and even the door frames. I tell her that we can come back in the morning if she prefers. I always tell the women that, because, like I said, I'm a big guy with a beard and tattoos, and sometimes the women are afraid of me, and it is late at night.

Before I met Carly—that's my wife—I didn't realize that women might be afraid of me, but then Carly told me that. I took a good look in the mirror and figured she was right.

I've been big all my life, but I've never been a bully. When I started in school my dad told me that I shouldn't pick fights because I was bigger than most of the kids and could hurt them bad. He told me it was okay to defend myself, but not to pick fights. He also told me that I should never hit a girl, even if they hit me. I sure listened to my dad, and I never had any problems. Except for that one girl in grade five who kept calling me a moose. That sure made me upset, but my mom told me to not show it and the girl would stop, because all she wanted was to get attention. So I did like my mom said, and she was right, and that girl and I even became friends when we went to high school. But I never had a fight, and I was glad my dad taught me that.

Carly will tell you that I'm a teddy bear, that I wouldn't hurt a flea, and that I cried when Beth died in that movie *Little Women*. I generally wouldn't tell anyone that, but now that I'm telling this story I'm saying so, because I want to explain that that's the kind of person I am.

It's Vern you have to watch out for.

The woman at this last job is a little cranky from all her waiting, I can see that, and I don't blame her, but she tells me she waited this long, and she's got to go back to work tomorrow, she can't miss another day, so please just get going and do what we have to do. I ask if I can see where the hot water tank has to go, and she shows me in. The house is kind of old, but I can see right away that we won't have to remove any door frames here, although maybe one of the doors will have to come off. The only way we can know this is to get started, so I tell the woman, and she says to go ahead. I tell her also that my name is Joe, and it's Vern who will be helping me. She tells me her name is Marlena.

We get the tank on the dolly and get it into the house without a problem, but the door to the basement is a little small. We try a couple times to wedge it through without wrecking the paint or anything, but it becomes clear that it isn't going through. I tell Vern I'm going to the truck to get the tool box and remove the door. Right away, Vern starts to argue, saying the lady can repaint it if we scratch, and what can she do about it anyway, we're two men and she's just a woman.

"Maybe she has a big husband," I say, and that shuts Vern up.

When I get back in with the tool box, I can hear Vern yapping it up, and I don't like what I hear. It sounds like he's telling Marlena that her husband should be up checking out what we're doing because, after all, it's his house, ain't it? I get in there as fast as I can, talking loudly, hoping the lady can't hear what Vern is saying, but I can tell by her face that the damage has started. I shoot Vern a dirty look.

"What?" he smirks.

I get the door off and set it aside carefully, and we put the tank on the straps. Vern negotiates so he's the first to go down the stairs, the part I usually do. He wants to prove how strong he is. I'm not going to argue with him. I know from past experience that will be useless.

Well, we get the thing down the stairs and get it hooked up, and I go back up to replace the door while Vern lights the pilot.

The protocol now is that we show the home owner how the tank operates. It's one of the newer models, but really, it's still simple for the owner.

I call the lady to come down the stairs, addressing her as "Miss" because that's the polite way to do it. But I can see that Vern is itching.

"Bring a pen and paper so you can write the instructions down for your husband," Vern calls up to her.

When Marlena comes down the stairs her face is red, and her mouth in a straight line. She looks Vern in the eye and tells him that she owns the home, lives here by herself, and is perfectly capable of understanding the instructions.

"Yeah, I shoulda figured you wouldn't have a man," Vern says.

"What in hell is that supposed to mean?" Marlena says, her arms crossed.

"You're the kind of woman who thinks she's as good as a man any day. You're not that bad looking. Lose the superior attitude and you might be able to get a man."

I've had enough of Vern now, and tell him flat out to shut up. He's not too happy with that.

I explain the instructions to Marlena, give her the booklet, apologize again for the delay, and thank her for her patience.

But Vern can't let it go.

"Think you can remember those instructions?" he asks.

The lady has had it now, and I don't blame her, so I don't interfere.

"Listen, squirt," she says. "I'm a corporate lawyer. I oversee mergers and acquisitions while you lift things up and down stairs. Don't for one second think you're superior to me in any way, because it's obvious you aren't."

Calling Vern a squirt burns him bad, and his face turns scarlet. I practically push him out the door ahead of me. Vern gets in the driver's seat while I climb in the passenger side, but before I can say anything he jumps out again.

"Forgot something," he mumbles, and goes back to Marlena's house, his steps as long as he can make them. I figure Vern's going back to get in one last insult, but I'm just too damn tired to care now. Anyway, I guess Marlena can dish it out just as well as Vern does.

Marlena opens the door and, after a little hesitation, lets him in. A few minutes later, he comes back out with something in his hand. I'm relieved he comes out so quickly. He can't have done too much harm in those few minutes. Vern goes to the back of the truck. Something clunks as he throws it inside.

"Left the screw driver behind." He grunts as he gets back into the driver's seat.

"Yeah, sure," I mumble.

When I get home it's almost 1 a.m. Carly has left some food in the fridge for me. I've told her several times that she doesn't have to do that, she works all day as well, but she does anyway. I'm so tired, I just leave the food and go to bed.

The next day is Saturday, and I get to sleep in and don't get up till after 10 a.m. Carly has gone to yoga, and I eat the food she left me last night. I turn on the radio, which is my usual habit, and I'm scanning the newspaper when something on the radio catches my attention.

There's been a gas explosion in a house. I think I catch the street, but I'm not sure. I get real fidgety because I think the street name they said is the street where we did the last service call. Marlena's street.

I start to leaf through the paper to see if there is anything there, but of course the paper probably came out before the explosion happened. Now I switch to a news station to see if I can catch some news, but I'm so nervous that I keep switching stations back and forth when I don't hear anything. Finally I get lucky and catch the news piece, and, oh my god, it *is* the street we were on, Marlena's street. One person is seriously injured, in emergency care in St. Joe's.

Vern, please tell me you didn't do anything last night – turn off the pilot light or something.

Then I feel like a total shit for thinking like that. But, I've worked with Vern a long time, and I know what he's capable of.

When Carly comes home, I'm pacing the floor, and she knows right away something is wrong. But I can't, I just can't, tell her about it, because what am I going to do? I tell Carly instead that I'm going out for a walk.

Carly has met Vern a couple times and doesn't particularly like him, but in a more neutral way. I mean, she doesn't out and out hate him, like some women he's insulted. Carly is a small woman, so she's not threatening to Vern, and she's wise enough to let his remarks slide off her shoulders, so Vern is okay with her, because she can't be bothered challenging him.

I'm trudging down the street heading for the lake and I'm thinking over my options. If Vern turned off that pilot light when he went back in, that's criminal. He'll go to jail. If that happens, he's gonna be in trouble among all those hardened criminals. For sure he's gonna be someone's girlfriend, or pretty boy, or whatever they get called. That's a nasty life for someone who doesn't want that kinda thing. But if he did turn off that pilot light he condemned someone else to a terrible life. Is it Marlena in emergency? Is she gonna be scarred for life? Is she even gonna be alive?

It's like I'm balancing one life against another life.

I don't normally swear that much, but I suddenly realize that I'm tramping down the street muttering "oh shit, oh shit". loud enough that the two girls coming towards me are getting afraid and turning into the nearest house prepared to bang on the door and get someone to save them from this huge, insane man. I figure I better go home before the police get calls about me.

When I get home, Carly tells me that Vern has called a couple times.

I make a decision. I'm calling the police. I've always been a responsible type person, and I'm not changing that now.

But first I tell Carly the whole story. Carly, bless her, tells me we're going for a car ride. We need to make sure it's the right address. Thank God I listen to her, because when we get near the street I can see the explosion is almost two blocks from Marlena's house. I guess on the way over I was holding my breath, because when I see it isn't the address we worked on, I let it all out and take in a healthy lung-full.

I've had enough of Vern.

When we get in the truck on Monday morning, I'm driving.

"Hey, didja see the game," Vern asks. "I tried to call you a couple times, but Carly said you weren't home."

I don't answer.

"Aaaah," Vern says. "You didn't get any last night, so now you're in a bad mood. Look at me; I'm in a good mood."

To listen to him you'd think he gets laid twice a day, every day.

I go into this big industrial plaza in the north part of the city. I drive into the back, behind the stores, where the garbage bins are. Vern looks puzzled, then terrified when I go round to his door and yank him out of the truck.

"Hey, hey, hey! What's got into you?" he yells, as I shove him up against the hood of the truck. I don't answer. I pick him up by the front of his jacket and shake him. I don't realize how angry I am. I shake him a few more times and yell right into his face.

"No more," I tell him. "Don't you ever fucking insult another woman when you're around me. When we go into anyone's house, you keep your mouth shut. And I mean shut the whole time. People are gonna think you can't talk. Do you understand me?"

I shake him again, because it looks like he's going to yap at me, or make excuses or something like that.

"Do you understand? Because if you don't you're going into that garbage bin with the other rats."

Finally, Vern just nods, and I let him down. We both go around and get into the truck.

"Jeeze," Vern mutters. "You'd think making a joke was a federal offense."

I shoot him a look and he stares out of his side window.

I'm still kind of shaking when I take the wheel. I don't like this feeling, and I'm glad my dad taught me the right thing. But I also know that if my dad were here now, he would think I did the right thing this time.

The Strap

IT'S MONDAY AFTERNOON, AND ALL the grades are working on what we call "The War Project".

The parents will complain about this, I know. I've been told more than once that my job is to teach the kids reading, writing and arithmetic. This is what the farmers want their kids to know, that and which cows are the best milkers, how to rotate crops, and, if you're a girl, how to obey and get dinner. Still, we are halfway through April, and I will risk the complaints. I think it is important for the children to know what is going on in the world, even if the parents don't think so.

Grade 5 created the map, drawing the continents carefully from the school atlas, and they are rightfully proud of their creation. The map takes up a good part of the side wall.

Grade six will keep track of the war efforts and colouring in the map – blue for the Allies, red for the Axis, and green for countries that declare neutrality. I have emphasized that the colours must be done lightly, so that the names can still be read. The first Canadian troops entered Europe in December, and the children gleefully, fearfully, coloured Canada blue.

Grade seven will be tracking significant events on the home fronts of the Allies – rationing, changes in the age for conscription, and civilian contributions toward the effort.

Grade eight is responsible for recording significant— soon to be historical—events, the most difficult chore, for who is to know which advance, which battle, which treaty, will be the most important in the end.

There is much excitement about Canada entering the war effort.

Michael, 15, and in grade eight, has declared that he will join the army as soon as they'll take him. Michael is big for his age and is the ringleader of the boys. His misdemeanors are well known in this small farming community: the snake in the school cupboard, the bird let loose in the boys' washroom, tossing the swing seat over the bars so that the swing is so high no child can reach it. The girls and the smaller boys avoid him on the playground. Every spring and fall he misses school to help with the sowing and harvesting, and so he has failed two grades.

I was warned about Michael when I started with this school in September, and advised by the superintendent to use the strap with him. "He'll get the belt from his father when he gets home if you use the strap, and that will deter him from a lot of mischief," Mr. Henderson said.

In my four years of teaching, I have never used the strap on a child. I don't believe in it. How can we tell children that hitting is wrong, and then hit them. We would end up teaching that "might makes right", that bullying works if you are bigger, or have more power. No, corporal punishment is not for me.

I can't say I haven't been tempted with Michael; he is certainly trying my patience. Bringing live mice to school and tossing them at the girls was his last misdemeanour and resulted in hysterics from Maud, Jean, and little Becky. Lizzie, Michael's sister, knew better than to show any fear. I made Michael write out pages from the dictionary every day during the lunch hour, for two weeks. I have to say he did it well and with a cheerful manner. I suppose it was little enough compared to the labour he is used to.

At 4:30 p.m. I walk back to the boarding house with Moira Hill, who teaches grades one to four in the other classroom. Miss Hill has only a high school education, but she talks about going on to "normal school". Otherwise, she will probably only be allowed to teach the lower grades.

Education values are changing in Ontario, and eventually even the rural areas will become part of the changes.

Miss Hill tells me how Vernon, grade 1, decided to decorate his face with his new crayons instead of using them to circle the largest number on his arithmetic work sheet. She laughs as she describes his black handle bar moustache and unibrow, and his bright red cheeks and lips. Vernon is still chubby with baby fat, and Miss Hill says that she could barely keep a straight face as she ordered him to go the washroom and wash his face.

Miss Hill is only nineteen, and will probably not teach for long. She is already being courted by Milt Sweet over on the next concession. I, on the other hand, am twenty five and considered a spinster.

But I have my secrets, and they make me smile to myself. I'm not as spinsterish as these folks think I am. Charlie Peters has come calling three times now in the last four weeks.

Charlie is a confirmed bachelor at 36, and never has much to say, so I am left to make up the conversation. But that, I know, is how these farmers are. And most men, I guess.

We take a walk down the lane, and sometimes through the meadow. Charlie helps me over the fence and his hand lingers on my waist. I know he likes my womanly figure. After the walk, I make us some lemonade, and we sit on the porch swing.

Next time he comes calling, I will let him kiss me. I'm not entirely ignorant of the womanly arts.

And the most delicious part is that last night, Miss Hill was home to see that I had a suitor too. Surprise, Miss Hill.

Tuesday is a warm day, and the children are possessed by the devil. Even Isobel is gazing wistfully out the window. By mutual agreement, Miss Hill and I have extended the morning recess by a few minutes. After all, 15 minutes is not much time for vigorous children to run off their energy.

Miss Hill comes to my classroom during the recess and looks around to make sure none of the children are being kept in.

"Miss Lee," she says. "Can we talk?"

"Of course," I reply.

I'm glad that Moira Hill knows I have a suitor. She can't lord it over me any longer.

But she seems unable to get started.

"Come, come," I say to her, as if I were talking to one of the children.

"It's about Charlie Peters," Miss Hill says, and stops again.

I purse up my lips and puff out a breath of impatience.

"Charlie's not like other men," Miss Hill says in a rush. "He's, he's different. You're not from around here, so you don't know."

Miss Hill turns an unbecoming dull red.

"Charlie likes other men."

"Well, I'm sure other men like Charlie," I say.

"That's not what I mean. I mean that Charlie likes men in the way that most men like women." She hesitates again. "There was some scandal a few years ago. Mr. Millsap saw him when he went into the city, and Charlie was going into one of those places. You know, those places where, where, uuumh, different men get together. Now Milt says he wants to get married so other people will think he is normal. But he isn't normal."

This is a deliberate attempt by Miss Hill to shame me. It's obvious she's jealous.

"Get out of my classroom," I say evenly.

"Please," she says. "It's not fair that he's trying to use you. I just don't want you to get hurt."

"Get out of my classroom," I repeat.

How dare she imply that Charlie only likes me to cover up his past? He likes me for real, as any man likes a woman. How dare she?

After recess, we are working on the map. I have my back turned to the class. I'm afraid that something will show on my face. I am watching Jack write the rationing quotas in England on the board. Canadian rationing is already on the board, and the children are doing some comparisons. Goods rationed are much the same, sugar, butter, tea, and I'm going to initiate a discussion as to why these goods are rationed. I'll let the children take the lead. Right now, I find it hard to concentrate on anything. Then I hear Michael's voice, a low undertone meant to be concealed by the soft chatter. I can't believe what I hear.

"Fat ass," Michael says. His best friend, Jimmy, snickers. I feel heat spreading up my neck and into my face, but I'm so angry I don't care.

"Michael," I say sharply, "stay in at lunch." He smirks at my red face, my aggravation.

When the children go out to play after lunch, Michael stays in. I call him to my desk and take out the strap. The smirk drops off his face.

"Miss Lee," Michael says, "when my father sees I got the strap, he'll beat me." I know it's not me he's afraid of, but his father. This enrages me more.

"You should have thought of that before," I say.

"But Miss, he'll really beat me. He's mad all the time since my mom died and he just looks for reasons to hit me. Last time, I had marks across my back for the longest time."

"You should have thought of that before," I repeat. I look him straight in the eye. "And Michael, if you pull your hand away I will go to your father myself and tell him why you're in trouble." He turns white. I had never seen him look scared before, and I feel like I am finally in command. It's a good feeling.

Michael's palm is brown, his hands already thickening with hard work.

The first strike leaves a red mark that covers his hand and up his wrist. I move to the side and hold his wrist.

I strike again and again. I don't look at Michael's face. I count. Seven, eight, nine, ten. As the strap comes down his hand changes from brown to pink, then to red. On strike number eight I see miniscule drops of blood, oozing. I continue. After the 10 strikes Michael's hand is bright red. It looks warm, heated.

"Left hand," I say.

I glance briefly at Michael. He is staring straight ahead, his face without expression. But tears stand in his brown eyes. I feel pleasure. There is no doubt about it. I feel pleasure. And I still have the left hand to do, 10 strokes.

The afternoon passes quietly, the children are subdued. I had promised a spelling bee for all the grades, but go next door and let Miss Hill know that it is cancelled. None of the children mention it. I think of Mr. Henderson's recommendation, and decide he's right. The strap is the answer.

The walk home that evening is quiet. Miss Hill ventures once to ask if I ever got the strap myself. I know she could hear me hitting Michael from the other class room. I don't answer. She doesn't say more, except to remark that spring is pretty much here.

The next day Michael isn't in school, and Lizzie doesn't have a note from their father.

"Where's Michael?" I ask.

"I don't know, Miss" Lizzie says. "He started out with me, but then he went into the woods by the Miller's place. His back is really sore, Miss Lee. My dad hit him with the buckle end of the belt. I heard him crying last night when he thought everyone was asleep, and he couldn't lean his back against the chair at breakfast this morning." She looks at me reproachfully.

"That will do, Liz" I say, and she sits back down.

We all recite the Lord's Prayer, and then I direct the grades to open their arithmetic books, and I assign pages. I direct grade five to study the seven and eight times tables. In 15 minutes I will quiz them on these tables while the other three grades work independently.

I look around the classroom and see Jimmy, grade seven, staring at me. He drops his eyes when I look back. I remember how he snickered yesterday, when Michael made his remark. I could have got him too, I think. He did snicker. That was probably worth at least three per hand.

Jimmy's hand would not be hardened like Michael's. His father doesn't farm; he works in the hardware store in town.

Jimmy wouldn't do farm chores; his hand would be soft and pink.

"I'll get you," I think with anticipation, with satisfaction. "Sooner or later I'll get you"

Dreaming

THE LITTLE HILL IS PERFECT. It's about three and a half feet high, and has a slight slope. Two little girls in worn cotton dresses lie on the hill, their feet braced at the bottom, and watch the clouds.

The sky is deep blue. Across the creek the cows make their way slowly toward a distant barn. No sound breaks the silence.

It is two weeks into summer vacation. Endless days of possibilities lie ahead.

"What colour is your dress?" asks Emma.

"Blue," says Rose. "See the sky in between those two biggest puffy clouds? It's just that colour, and it has white swans down all around the neck and the hem. What colour is your dress?"

"Oooh," breathes Emma. "Your dress is beautiful. My dress is pale pink, with pale blue swans down around the neck and hem."

"You can't have blue swans down," says Rose.

"Why not?"

"Well, did you ever see a blue swan."

"I never even saw a white swan," says Emma.

Rose glances quickly at her sister. "Well, we could probably dye the swans down," she says.

"Yeah, we could dye it. You can dye just about anything." Emma giggles and nudges Rose with her elbow. "Remember when Mom dyed her hair that yellow colour, and Daddy got so mad and said she looked like an old horse?"

"I remember," replies Rose. She thinks for a minute. "I don't think he said 'horse', though. I think he said a different word."

"Well, what do you think he said? It sure sounded like 'horse' to me."

"I don't know, but Mom got so mad, I think he said something else. There sure was a lot of yelling that time."

Emma digs her toe into the dirt at the bottom of the hill to keep from sliding down. Dirt sifts into the hole in her runner and grits on her foot. She expertly points her toe and shakes her foot, and sand trickles back out of the hole.

"And my dress will have sequins on it too, like that dress in the Eaton's catalogue." "Sequins and swans down."

Behind the girls a door opens and a woman throws water from a tin wash basin into the yard.

"Rosie and Emmie, you two get in this house and get these dishes done," the woman calls.

"Okay, Mom," Rose replies.

After a comfortable silence of some minutes, Emma asks, "But what will the men wear?"

Rose considers. "Maybe they would wear what that man wore in the poem Miss Phillips read to us. You know, that man who rode around robbing people on the highway. He wore a coat of some kind of velvet, and lace underneath his chin, and big tall boots."

"Oh Rose, men don't wear lace."

Both girls know this is true.

"Well, maybe it was the girl that wore the lace," Rose says. "I'm gonna' have lace on my dress, and it'll be in a sort of 'V' shape in the front and the back."

"You don't want everyone to see your boosums, do you Rose?"

"I haven't got any boosums."

The girls giggle.

"But you'll have them when you grow up," says Emma. "Who knows, maybe they'll be as big as the minister's wife's boosums."

The girls turn their heads simultaneously towards each other, and grin. Emma's grin is gap-toothed.

Their conversation is interrupted by a boy about six years old. He wears cut-down coveralls with the legs rolled up unevenly. He has a plane made out of two pieces of wood nailed clumsily together. He runs around the girls and flies his plane closer and closer to their heads.

"Stop that, Floydie," complains Emma.

Floyd ignores her, but as he zooms past, Rose calmly puts out a stick-thin leg and trips him. Floyd howls in indignation.

"You tripped me. I'm gonna tell."

"If you do, I'll get you back," Rose threatens.

Floyd thinks about this. Someday, he'll be bigger than his sisters, and he'll be able to beat up on them, but not yet. He makes a decision and zooms his plane down the lane-way.

The girls gaze placidly at the clouds.

"What will the ballroom look like, Rose?" asks Emma.

"Oh, it'll be huge. And it'll have one of those candeliers, you know, those lights that got a lot of bulbs that look like candles on them, and dangly things hanging down. Like in your old Cinderella book. And the walls will all be painted in nice colours, pink and yellow. And it'll be all decorated with balloons, hundreds of balloons. All colours. And with those paper streamers like Miss Phillips lets us put up for the Christmas Concert, all different colours twisted around each other. And some of the streamers will hang down. It will have a big, long staircase, and when me and you come down the stairs, the music and dancing will stop and everyone will look up at us 'cause we'll be so beautiful."

The girls smile happily at each other.

"Rosie and Emmie, you two git in this house." Their mom's voice calls out of the kitchen window behind them. But the two girls think only of the beautiful ballroom.

A little girl of about three, dressed in a soggy cloth diaper, comes and stands in front of them. Her thumb is stuck in her mouth. Her eyes are round and blue, her face placid, empty.

"Come here, Flora," says Rose. Flora sits down beside her. Rose crooks her arm around the child's waist. Flora gives a little sigh, and sucks her thumb.

"We'll have lots of good things to eat," says Emma. "We'll have some of that cake that the minister's wife makes and butter tarts like Mom makes for when Aunt Evelyn and Uncle Harvey comes over. Lots of chocolate."

"No turnips or beets," says Rose.

"Miss Phillips says that sometimes in the city they make deserts that look like other things, like maybe a cake that looks like a piano. We could have some of them. What would you want your cake to look like, Rose?"

"If you don't git in here and do these dishes, I'm gonna tell your dad," their mom hollers out the kitchen window .

Behind them, Floyd runs up and down the lane making zooming noises.

But the girls are lost in a lovely anticipation of the food.

"Maybe an animal. Maybe like one of them kittens that the Miller's got in their barn. Yeah, a white kitten," says Rose.

"Mr. Miller drowned those kittens," says Emma sadly. "He took them down to the creek in a bag and put a stone in the bag."

"I know. I think he likes to drown 'em." says Rose. "Don't you worry about it, Emma, 'cause you can't stop him."

All is silent. The sky is still blue, the air is soft. The clouds glide by.

A footstep sounds behind them. Emma springs suddenly to her feet, but Rose is too late. A large man dressed in coveralls and rubber boots grabs her by her upper arm and lifts her off the ground. Flora rolls out of her sister's arm, and down the little hill. Her diaper collects dirt and grass as she tumbles. Rose's short yellow dress hikes up, exposing a pair of greyish panties. Floyd, who has zoomed his plane back down the lane, sniggers.

"You girls git in that kitchen and help your ma," says the man.

"Yes, Daddy," both girls say.

Emma stands Flora on her feet and brushes some of the dirt from around her mouth and off her hands. Flora doesn't cry; she sticks her thumb back in her mouth.

"You git in that house too."

Flora totters after her sisters.

"Too much book readin'," declares the man.

"I don't read any books, Daddy," says Floyd.

"Course you don't, you're a boy."

Floyd smirks. He knows this is what gives him an advantage over his sisters. He knows that someday he will tell them what to do, and they'll have to do it because he'll be a man, and he'll be big. He zooms his plane back up the lane as his dad walks out to the pickup.

The girls' mother sits at the kitchen table drinking tea out of a chipped mug.

"I told you I'd git your dad after you," she says. "I hope he gave you a good clip across the head. Heat that kettle up again so you'll have some hot water for the dishpan. I swear, you two better learn to do some work, or you aren't ever going to get married and have a family. Who'd want to marry such lazy girls."

The two little girls keep their eyes down as they go about heating the dishwater and clearing the table. But underneath their lids they glance at each other in a silent communication. They know there are better things than marriage in their future.

Nothing Else to Say

"I'M GOING TO LIVE TO be a healthy ninety-nine, and then jump over a guard rail in front of an eighteen wheeler."

That's what I used to say. But I've had to revise that a bit. For one thing, I can't help worrying about the poor truck driver. His whole life will be affected if he hits a little old woman with his truck. It won't matter that I'm old, or that I was the one who jumped off the overpass, it will still be terrible for him. And if he has a wife and kids it will be terrible for them too. So, lately, I've started to think about a more humane way to do this. Humane for others, I mean, not for myself. For myself, I intend to be fast and thorough.

The other part I have to revise is the age. I'm 84 now, and I thought I was in excellent health for my age, but another aspect just presented itself. It started with balance. Or rather, the loss of balance. Well, I figured, I am getting older so I better do something about this. I put a post-it note with a stick figure on my bathroom mirror to remind myself to stand on one foot when brushing my teeth. It was supposed to be a painless way to practice my balance. It didn't turn out to be painless, since I lost my balance and fell, my hand going into the toilet, wrenching my shoulder. It could have been worse. I'm very glad I kept up with my fitness routine; some massage and cold packs, and extra rest, put me right.

But then I noticed that my hand was trembling and my thumb was rubbing my finger, seemingly without my control. That was strange. It was my shoulder I injured. I know everything is connected, like we sang in the old song when we were children, but this rubbing thing was odd. So, off I went to my doctor.

Parkinson's is a difficult disease to diagnose. There is no specific test, although some neurological tests certainly point the way. In the end, it is diagnosed through a series of symptoms and by eliminating other causes and/or diseases. That was how I was diagnosed.

Of course, I got on- line and I didn't like what I read at all. The part that really bothered me was what some articles referred to as Stage 3, officially called Bradykinesia and identified as a gradual degradation of movement. But the part that terrified me is that one can be moving freely one minute and completely unable to move the next. If I couldn't move at all, that truck driver has nothing to worry about.

I didn't intend to spend the rest of my life being spoon-fed, and, more horrifying, having the other end wiped. I needed to figure out a plan as soon as I could.

Back on line, I googled for painless ways to commit suicide and got 1,430,000 results in under a second. I was flabbergasted. I clicked on to a site called "Lost All Hope", and then on to a section titled "Your Stories". And I was saddened. There were stories of young men and women who had lost their marriages, people who were going through extended bad times, people who had tried and failed to end their life. Worst of all were stories from young people, 11 years old, 14 years old, feeling worthless, feeling depressed.

As a secondary school teacher for more than 40 years, I know how desperate young people can feel. They feel there is no hope left. I'm 84, and I will end my life somehow, but at least I have had a life. Fortunately many of the online stories were from those whose attempts had failed, who had decided to try to live again, and whose lives had become bearable, some even happy.

Another part of the web site listed ways to off oneself, how lethal each method was, how long it would take, and the agony factor. For sure I won't stab myself in the abdomen: it takes more than four hours to die and the agony factor is high. I looked up my old joke plan—jumping in front of a truck—70% lethal, 19 minutes to die, and an agony level of 63. My old joke didn't seem much of a joke now.

Many of those who failed in their attempt ended up seriously and/or permanently injured.

I was exhausted, and all I had done was peck away on the computer. Time for a cup of tea, and time for bed.

Today, I check out success statistics. In young people (aged 15 - 24), the odds are between 100 and 200 to 1 *against* success. The elderly seem a lot more successful at 4:1. I'm curious about this and so I read on. It seems that the elderly's success rate is because they are more certain they want to go through with it.

It isn't even noon yet, and I'm bushed. I decide that this research is just too emotionally distressing, and that's why I'm so tired. Or maybe it's the Parkinsons. I resolve to get to the heart of the matter right away, and click on a link for euthanasia and assisted suicides, and I find hope. The Dignitas Clinic in Switzerland offers assisted suicide. Swiss laws are among the most liberal as far as assisted suicides go.

Before I can research too much about the Swiss clinic, there's a banging on the door, then my Ellie's cheerful voice.

"Open up, Gran," she hollers.

I hurry downstairs to let her in before she hollers any more. In she breezes, asking me in a loud voice if I'm hiding my lover, or two lovers, or hiding some pot, and declaring she will search the house until she weeds out any illegal substances.

My Ellie is 23 now, but I remember her in grade five, furious and telling off her classmates for bullying a new kid in class, the son of an immigrant who didn't have the right clothes. And Ellie, being popular, was successful in his defense.

And I remember her in grade nine, cutting her beautiful dark hair short because she "couldn't deal" with all the fuss of putting it up for gym and tennis lessons.

Now, Ellie is trying to make her living as an actress and struggling to put food on her table while working at waitressing and temp work. When the next big break comes up, she will quit her day job and go off in pursuit of fame and fortune. Likely, it will be more fame than fortune, but she is good at thrift. Tall and boisterous, she is a light in my life, and confusion in her conservative mother's life.

She fills the kettle, chatting amiably, and asks if I have any muffins. I do, and also some of the lasagne I had for dinner last night, which she promptly sticks in the microwave. She makes her coffee, sits down, and shovels the food into her mouth.

"Gran, what are you doing with your thumb?" she asks.

I look at how my thumb is rubbing my finger and I put my right hand over my left hand, but to my alarm, that hand starts shaking.

"What's happening, Gran?" Ellie asks.

I sigh. "Parkinson's is happening, Ellie."

"Oh, Gran, no." Ellie reaches across the table and takes my hands in hers.

"I'm going to research online," she says. Despite all evidence to the contrary, young people believe that old people don't know how to use the internet.

"No, I've done that already," I say.

I tell her about Bradykinesia and about how terrified I am.

"Gran, I'll help. It's going to be okay," she says. I smile, thinking of all the times I've said that to my precious granddaughter: when she skinned her knee, when her mom was angry with her, when she fought with her best friend, when her live-in boyfriend left.

"It will be okay," I reply.

"I'm just going up to check my email," Ellie tells me, and bounds up the stairs. Too late, I realize, I've left the information about ways to commit suicide and about the clinic in Switzerland on the screen.

Ellie hollers down at me that I better not eat her muffin and then she is quiet. She is quiet for a long, long time. Normally, she would stomp back down the stairs, but this time she is so silent that I don't realize she is there and I'm startled to see her when I turn from the garbage where I am scraping the empty lasagna container.

"Gammy," she says. It is what she called me when she was a toddler and had difficulty with the 'r' sound. She stopped calling me that when she got into grade one and was told by the other six-year olds that it was a baby thing to say.

She puts her strong arms around me and hugs me.

"Gammy," she says again. "I've never been to Switzerland, and if you go, I want to go with you."

"Oh, Ellie, Ellie, thank you," I say.

Because, right at this moment, there is nothing else to say.

I Was Warned

THE OTHER KIDS DON'T PLAY with me much anymore. They used to. I used to be kind of popular. When I was little, the other parents would tell my mother that I was such a good looking boy with my curly blond hair and my blue, blue eyes.

But then one day, when I was making faces, my face got stuck that way. Now my tongue sticks out of my mouth on one side and my nose is kind of pushed up like a pigs snout, and my eyes are kind of pulled down so you can see the red part underneath.

"I told you so," my mother said.

Sometimes the littler kids are kind of scared of me.

I used to be pretty good at baseball. I was the catcher, or sometimes they put me out behind second base. But I'm not so good at that anymore. Now I just kind of throw the ball up against the wall and catch it. I have to do it all with one hand. That's why they don't let me play baseball anymore. My left hand is still okay; I can catch with that hand, but my right hand was my good throwing hand. Now my right hand is sort of stuck to my face, 'cause my finger got stuck up my nose. The other kids don't want to eat with me in the cafeteria anymore. They keep telling me I'm gross.

"I told you so," my mother said.

I play by myself a lot now.

Another reason why they won't let me play baseball (or hockey either, for that matter,) is because I don't see so good anymore. It's my peripal vision, or at least that's what the eye doctor called it. It happened when I was running, pretending I had a sword, and fell down. All this slimy white stuff came out of my eye and got on the end of the stick. It looked kind of like egg white. Now I just see out of my right eye, but it's kind of difficult because I got to turn my head to the left anytime I want to look in that direction, and my right hand kind of gets in the way too, because that's the hand where the finger is stuck up my nose.

"I told you so," my mother said.

After I poked my eye out, I stopped running with sticks for a while. but then I thought *What the heck, my eye is already poked out, so I'll just make sure I carry the stick in my left hand.* I couldn't hold anything in my right hand anyway. That worked for a while, but then, wouldn't you know it, I poked out someone else's eye.

"I told you so," my mother said.

Everyone got really upset with me that time, and I heard some people refer to me as a freak and say I should be put in a home. I couldn't figure that one out 'cause I already got a home, but a lot of the time it's hard to tell what grown-ups are talking about anyway.

The other thing that kind of affects my seeing, and why they don't let me play baseball anymore, is that my neck is kind of twisted to the right. That makes it even more difficult for my peripal vision. I don't remember too much of what happened that time, but I know that I spent a lot of time in the hospital after I fell out of that tree, and then for a long time I had to wear this big plastic thing around my neck. The doctor said it was a wonder I recovered, that I didn't become something that I can't remember the name of, but that means that I wouldn't be able to use my arms or legs again.

"I told you so," my mother said.

At least, that's what I think she said. My hearing hasn't been so good since that thing with the beans when I was just little. Anyway, that's what she usually says, so she probably said it again.

So, I been feeling real lonely lately.

Just this afternoon when I was walking home from school I thought maybe I had made a new friend. I had just about reached the big bridge that goes over the river when I noticed that this big car was kind of following behind me. I couldn't really see it, it was on my left side, my bad side, but I could hear it. I was feeling so bad I didn't even look around, although I heard it following me for a while. Then I heard the window roll down. The cars today got electric windows so that the driver can roll down the window on the other side, or roll it up if he wants. Then I heard this man say to me "Hey kid, want some candy?"

I didn't even look at the man, I was so glad that someone wanted to be my friend, and was going to give me candy into the bargain. I just hopped right into his car. The man started to drive the car real fast over the bridge, and he wasn't looking at me at first. Then he looked at me, and he said, "Hey kid, get your finger out of your nose, or I'm not gonna give you any candy."

So I turned around to explain that I couldn't get my finger out of my nose, and this guy kind of freaked out. He pulled the car right over to the curb and ordered me to get out. I think he called me a freak too, but I couldn't tell for sure. Anyway, it seemed like this guy didn't really want to be my friend after all. I asked for the candy, but he practically pushed me out of the car and then he peeled out.

I feel kind of bad that this guy didn't want to be my friend either, but really, it's going to be okay. At school today, I heard Johnny say that he was going to jump in the river, and it's only a short walk back to the bridge.

Party Story

THE LITTLE GET-TOGETHER THAT *got out-of-hand,*
Beth thinks. She is in the kitchen, checking on the lasagna. In
her apartment is a gathering of women, about half of whom
she doesn't know.

It started when she invited Marie to her annual Christmas
gathering. Marie had asked whether she could bring her sister,
Rita. Rita was new to the city, and did not yet have any
friends. Beth had, of course, agreed.

Then she asked Marion from work, who had recently
"come out," and Marion refused to attend without her
partner, Rachel. That was fine with Beth. She had never met
Rachel, but Marion was a congenial, good-hearted person, so
Rachel was welcome.

Beth had mentioned this development to the third person
she invited. Tina declared, "the more the merrier", and said
she would bring a friend, Sylvia. Sylvia, she stated, was
flamboyant and would liven up any get together.

After that, Beth gave up and told her remaining friends,
Amelia, Patti, and Maggie, to bring a woman friend as well, if
they liked.

Now, twelve women—six friends, and six friends-of-
friends—are gathered in her apartment. Beth, a conscientious
hostess, is making an effort to attach the correct name to the
correct face for each of the six strangers.

Beth picks up a bottle of wine and moves into the dining
room where the nibbles are. She goes over to join Amelia at
the snacks.

As Amelia lifts a shrimp on a cracker, a woman on the
other side of the table says, "You don't really need those
calories, do you? You'd be better off with a celery stick."

Beth looks with amazement at the woman who has
spoken. She is a small, beige, nondescript woman. Amelia

pauses, the cracker halfway to her lips. "An ounce on the lips, a pound on the hips," says the small beige woman.

Amelia, always conscious of her hips, returns the cracker to the plate and excuses herself to the washroom.

The small beige woman strolls into the other room. Beth, aghast, stares after Amelia. She wonders if this woman is Amelia's friend.

After uncorking the wine, Beth goes into the living room to mingle. She joins a small group where Tina is telling a story.

"Well, when I found a dead mouse in the basement, I put out mouse poison," Tina recounts. "I put out that seed that kills mice by dehydrating them. Then three weeks later, my basement flooded. When I saw all that water down there, I was afraid to go down. I was afraid I would be confronted by a battalion of re-hydrated mice bent on revenge."

The women laugh, except for the small beige woman. She is staring at Sylvia.

"What's all that black stuff around your eyes?" says the small beige woman to Sylvia. "Didn't you take off your make-up before you went to bed last night?"

The women are thunderstruck, bamboozled. They gape at one another. Tina stands up to defend her friend.

"Your house can't be very clean if you've got mice," says the small beige woman to Tina.

The women's mouths open and closes silently. The small beige woman wanders away.

Tina follows Beth out to the kitchen to help with the food. "Who's friend is she?"

"I don't know, but I wish they'd take her home," Beth whispers back.

The two women, joined by others, bring out the food.

The small beige woman is first in line, and she fills her plate. Beth is glad she has prepared generously.

As the women crowd into the room and begin to eat, several praise Beth's lasagna.

"Have you tasted the President's Choice lasagna?" the small beige woman asks. "It beats out the home-made stuff any day."

Several women defend Beth's lasagna, but the small beige woman appears not to hear. She is engrossed in eating.

Uncomfortable minutes pass as Beth searches her mind for conversation. Finally, she asks Maggie how her pregnancy is going. Maggie cheerfully advises the women that this has been an easy pregnancy.

"A bad sign," says the small beige woman. "When the pregnancy is easy, there's usually something wrong with the fetus."

The conversational attempt comes to an abrupt halt. The other women all stare at the small beige woman.

As with one mind, they wish that whoever brought her would have the sense to remove her.

"Well, got to run," says the small beige woman.

She picks out several chocolates from the gift box one of the guests has brought as a hostess gift for Beth, gets her coat, and leaves.

No one goes with her.

Beth looks around in amazement. She counts twelve guests.

Persevere

SHARON LOOKS FOR THE PARKING spot closest to the hospital door, and, seeing nothing else, parks in the wheel chair spot. *I can justify that.*

She heads down the hall, greets a familiar nurse with a friendly smile, and marches onward to the oncology unit. The receptionist is busy checking someone in, but nods towards the washroom door. Sharon knocks.

Kelly calls out, "Just a minute," and takes measure of herself in the mirror as she washes her hands. Her skin is pale, her hair, which she had cut soon after beginning treatment, is growing dryer and thinner. Her eyes look huge. *There's one compensation.* She smiles as she remembers her adolescent self striving for that big eyed look. Well, she has that look now. They could paint her on black velvet.

Her stomach rolls, and she bends over the toilet bowl again and retches. She still has some fluid in her stomach to bring up, and is glad she follows the advice to drink lots of liquids on the day before and on the day of the chemo. But now she's developed sores in her mouth, and anything citric is out. Too bad. Kelly loves those little clementines you get at Christmas. She will check her resource booklet for soothing foods. She washes her hands again, rinses her mouth, and leaves the washroom.

"How you doing, kiddo?" Sharon asks. She takes her friend's sharp elbow, but changes her grip as she feels Kelly tremble. With her arm around her friend's waist, she walks Kelly toward the exit.

Outside, a man in a security guard uniform is walking around her car. He starts to say something, then he takes a look at Kelly, gives a little salute, and goes to the back of the car to direct them out.

Freezing rain coats the windows, and the defroster has a hard time keeping up. Sharon takes it slowly. "I hate city driving," she says, and Kelly nods. She knows Sharon can't see her nod, and doesn't need to. They are on the same wave length.

They have been friends for almost 40 years, played together as infants, snuggled to sleep together when their mothers visited. At the age of eight, they cut their fingers with a small jackknife and mingled their blood. Neither of them knew how much it would hurt, and Kelly, who was first because it was her idea, yelled. But Sharon, always the braver one, went ahead anyway. At nine, on a sleep-over, they had their first big disagreement, something about Barbie dolls. At fifteen, they had a falling out for a week, over a boy, of course. It was Sharon who called Kelly that time. "Kell," she said, "is he worth it?"

"No" said Kelly, instantly.

Sharon is auntie to Kelly's three children, has taught them to play poker, and taken them on trips Kelly couldn't possibly afford. John Peter, called JP by everyone, is fourteen now. When he is with his friends, he calls a brief "Hi, Aunt Sharon", but at home he is always ready to sit down to a game of penny poker. Trevor, 12, and Lisa, 10, still dote on their aunt and clamor for her attention when she comes to visit. Sharon is fascinated with their growth, with JP now being almost a young man, and Trevor with his voice starting to crack. She braids Lisa's long brown hair, invents new hair styles for her.

Sharon loves being with them, but nevertheless is always glad to go back to her quiet, childless life.

Kelly has seen Sharon through her divorce from Richard. She had wished Sharon out of the relationship long before Sharon did, but managed to keep her mouth shut. It was a very difficult thing, to keep her mouth shut when she saw her friend being hurt, but she only repeated to Sharon that she would be there if Sharon ever needed anything.

No, words were not needed.

They have reached Hwy. 401 now, and the going is easier. The passing of countless cars has dried the asphalt. Sharon picks up speed.

"I'll make you some soup, or something, when we get home," she offers.

"That would help," Kelly says.

There is silence.

"Sharon, you'll take care of Lisa, won't you?" Kelly says. "Oh, I know you will, I don't have to keep saying it. It's just that she's the one I worry about the most. Her dad will look out for her, but you know, a girl needs to have a woman around to talk to. And, maybe, to talk to John too, if he gets over protective. John does respect your opinion."

"I know. You say it if you have to. And I promise I'll be there for her if ever I'm needed. No matter what. But, Kell, I'm not going to be needed. You're going to be there for Lisa. You'll be there to help her through those teenage years and see her get married, if that's what she wants. The radiation, the chemo, it's all working. The doctor said so. You're going to get better."

They are at the turnoff to the secondary road that will take them home. This is a drive they both love in the spring and the fall. The hills undulate, the view widens and narrows as they crest and drop. As children, going to the city with one set of parents or the other, they would close their eyes, the better to feel the lift and swoop.

Today, the road is treacherous. Sharon grips the wheel a little tighter and slows down.

"Kell," she says, "one more treatment, and then everything will get better. One more treatment. Kell, you can grow out your beautiful hair again, you'll be able to taste again. We'll go for Greek. We'll eat popcorn, drink wine, get tipsy, and laugh like a couple of fools again. It'll be good."

Kelly turns her head and smiles at her friend. "It'll be good," she echoes.

The car is going a little fast down the hill, but Sharon doesn't touch the brake. Braking on this ice would only cause a slide. She has driven these roads all her adult life, and knows how to do it.

"Kell," she says. "We're going to a spa this spring. My treat. For your birthday. We'll get facials. And massages. I'm going to find us a spa where the masseuse is 6 foot, 200 pounds, with big hands. Big hands."

Kelly giggles. Something in Sharon's chest jumps up, a little leap of hope, or joy.

"Almost home."

They crest the next hill. As they start down they see it coming down the hill in front of them. An eighteen wheeler. The trailer is swinging out from the side of the cab, overtaking the cab. It slithers sideways, the cab tips, and the trailer is in command. It swings and slides. In spite of the ice slicked road, sparks fly up where the cab is being dragged. The back of the trailer catches up to the front of the trailer, and the whole thing thunders down the hill sideways.

Sharon wrenches the wheel to the left, and the car starts to spin, out of control.

In the seconds left, as if with one brain, both women have the same thought.

"Christ, all that fucking chemo for nothing."

Dear Diary

JAN 1

Dear Diary: I can't believe how many years I've been doing this. When I was a kid it wasn't cool, but now it's called journaling, so I guess that makes it acceptable. My wishes for this year are mundane: health and happiness.

JANUARY 21

Dear Diary: A difficult but rewarding day at volunteer work. Spent an hour with G. who will be leaving two small children behind. She had to tell me (or just someone) all about the cute little things they do, how the oldest is doing in school, how she thinks the youngest will have difficulty sitting still. Of course, then she started to cry knowing she will never know how he does do in school Gave her a back rub after a while, and she fell asleep exhausted by emotion. Very difficult to hear, but I know I did good in the world today. On a more cheerful note, had a great time at euchre last night. The four of us spent more time laughing about the past then playing cards.

FEBRUARY 3

Dear Diary: Ridiculous. I forgot the kettle on the stove, and Josie made a huge fuss. Now, she's determined that she's getting me an electric kettle with an automatic shut off. The girl always was a drama queen. Although she *was* really good as a Lady Macbeth in that high school play. James and I were certainly proud of that—attended every time. Of course, she, Peter and the boys arrived on my euchre night, saying they were here for just a short visit, and what a rush to get ready after that. I think she thinks my time is free, or wasted, now that I'm finally retired. She doesn't know how wrong she is.

Had a good night at euchre, though. Belle was really ticked. Pleases me.

FEBRUARY 13
Dear Diary: Had a call from Patty today. She says she's doing well in the big city. Sure hope so. If she wasn't, I would be the last to know.

FEBRUARY 27
Hell of a day. Mariette called me into her office today and tried to convince me I needed a vacation from my volunteering. Told me what a great worker I was, but that right now they had more volunteers than they needed, and I should wait for a call before I came back. I said if I was so good, why were they telling me to quit? M. said someone had seen me giving medication to a patient. What a crock! The woman had a headache, so I gave her a tylenol. Does it take a doctor. to prescribe that? To top it all off, had a bad night at euchre. I trumped Mary Beth's bower a couple times, so she wanted to know what was wrong with me. I told her what happened, but made her promise not to tell anyone else.

MARCH 5
Dear Diary: Turns out, Mary Beth can't keep her mouth shut, and here comes Josie asking me what happened at the hospital. Told her she wasn't her mother's keeper, and she left in a huff, saying she was only trying to help me. I relented later and called her to say I was sorry.

MARCH 9
Dear Diary: Since I have free time on my hands now, decided to get into better shape and took a long walk. Must have been thinking about all this crap and got lost. When I came out of my fog, I didn't know where I was, and had to ask a man who was watering his lawn. It turned out that I was only a few blocks from home, and you would think I would recognize

the streets since I've been living here for more than twenty years. I guess that comes from always having a car.

MARCH 12
Sure do miss the hospital work.

MARCH 22
Don't know what happened this morning. Decided to take a long walk but was still in my pajamas. The police picked me up, called Josie, and said I'd been wandering. Embarrassing. I must have too much on my mind.

APRIL 1
Dear Diary: Patty came to visit. Says she's got a week's vacation. I'm so happy to see her. Of my three, I always thought it would be her who would have a hard time settling down. I was right. And now that makes me think of G. and her having to leave her two behind.

APRIL 3
Dear Diary: Even the good apple has a worm in it. Turns out Patty has been talking to Josie. They think I'm getting senile, because I can't find my keys sometimes. Anyway, I'm not going to ruin Patty's visit, I'll just keep quiet. We did go to a great restaurant. I have to say, Patty knows how to

APRIL 19
Dear Diary: Missed my euchre last night. Can't think how that happened.

APRIL 22
Dear Diary: Last night was

APRIL 30
Dear Diary: Josie wants me to see a doctor. I reminded her that I had my checkup on my birthday, and I was fine. She

wants me to discuss my forgetfulness with the dr. Everyone forgets some things.

MAY 3
MB claims I've been trumping her bowers again. She was nice enough about it, took me aside and said she was concerned about me, but the reality is that she's never been a very good player and now wants to blame it on me. Just told her I would be more careful. She's been a friend for a lot of years, and I don't want to hurt her feelings.

MAY 12
Dear Diary: I went to the dr. to satisfy Josie. I had another little episode of not watching where I was walking and getting lost. Although this time I managed to get dressed first. Afterwards, the doctor talked to Josie, as if suddenly I wasn't able to talk for myself. Pissed me off.

MAY 17
Dear Diary: Quit euchre. Let them find another player.

MAY 28
Dear i don't know

JUNE 5
Dear Diary: Now, I am getting scared. Ran into Josie in the grocery store and couldn't figure out who she was for a minute. Don't know what I was writing about on May 28th. Must have been interrupted in the middle of it.

JUNE 7
Jimmy called. Said he just wanted to know how I was. Told him I was fine. Told him I would love to see him & Liza and my granddaughters some day.

JUNE 18
Dear Diary: Caught Josie looking at this diary today. When I confronted her, she said she was worried about me. Who the hell does she think she is sticking her nose into my business?

JULY 3
Dear Diary: I took much today, and boy, didn't fear a thing.

JULY 4
Dear Diary: Had to admit I'm having problems with memory and started on some pills yesterday. Spent most of the day on the toilet, or bending over it.

JULY18
Dear Diary: I gave those pills a good try. They make me sick and sure don't cure me forgetfulness.

AUGUST 3
Can't believe some of the things that's been happening. Can't beli

AUGUST 44
Dear don't know whats happening to me

AUGUST 45
Dear Daar

SEPT
Dear Dairy I couldn't figure out where I was when I woke up this am. Wandered around for a bit then i saw a phone # in big letters by the phone. As soon as I heard Josie's voice, I came to myself. Josie coming over after work. Thank God.

Dear Daisy I'm so confused Didn't know where I was today. Some wioman who was cleeening said I was in Safe Haven. When i went tot he door there were all these strange people walking up up the hallway i want josie. i think i kept calling for her but she didn't

josie wher

The Writing Workshop

NIGHT SCHOOL DID NOT GO well for Ethan that evening.

This is what happened.

The beauteous Ms. Riley did not sit in her accustomed seat. Ms. Riley usually sat near the end of the table next to Mr. Gibaharldimaxima, but tonight she chose to sit beside Ethan. As soon as Mr. G. saw what was happening, he rose hastily and began to make his way around the side of the table. He intended to occupy the chair on the other side of Ms. Riley, where, seated by her side, his short stature would allow him to appreciate her bountiful nature. However, he was thwarted in his mission by the arrival of Miss Gertrude Peavy, who made her way to his end of the table, effectively blocking his passage. As The Instructor took his usual place at Mr. G's immediate left, and several other class members hurried in, his route was cut off, and he sank grumpily into his chair. Ethan, in the meantime, was trying to deal with the unnerving presence of Ms. Riley and the overpowering fragrance of her Cinnamon Meadows perfume. His eyes began to itch.

Miss Peavy's story was the first to be critiqued that evening. Mrs. Goodwind did the initial critique. The group usually afforded Mrs. Goodwind that particular right, as Mrs. Goodwind was a Published Author. A few years ago, while living in the village of Twood (population 800), Mrs. Goodwind had published several items in the local newspaper. Two articles were detailed descriptions of local Tupperware parties; the third was a wonderful description of a wedding shower that had been given for a rural couple. While the items were not strictly fiction, at the first meeting, Mrs. Goodwind had kindly provided copies for each group member as examples of "Show, don't Tell."

"Gertrude," Mrs. Goodwind said, referring to her notes, "your story does not have a plot. This is the third chapter of this story that we have critiqued, and it still does not have a plot."

"Ah, but Mrs. Goodwind," interrupted Mr. Gibaharldimaxima, "the descriptions are wonderful. Listen to this. This is most certainly the 'line of the week'. And Mr. Gibaharldimaxima read: 'Holly shivered in fear and anticipation as Lance displayed his magnificent weapon. As she tossed and turned on the bed in a helpless effort to free herself, her little satin chemise began to slide down, exposing her full, round breasts to Lance's burning gaze.'

"Beautiful, beautiful." murmured Mr. G. thoroughly transfixed by Miss Peavy's writing skills. Miss Peavy, who had begun to write after her retirement from accounting, smiled complacently. She knew she could always count on Mr. Gibaharldimaxima for a good, honest critique. The lack of plot did not bother her in the least.

Several other group members gave feedback on the story. The general consensus was that the descriptions were good, but that the story did lack a plot.

At the end, as was the custom, it was The Instructor's turn to comment.

"Gertrude," said The Instructor, leaning forward to allow the full wisdom of his words to impress the group members. "Your story lacks a plot. And furthermore..." The Instructor paused for dramatic effect, but unfortunately he paused too long. Several group members wondered if he had lost his train of thought, or even fallen asleep. However, they maintained a respectful silence.

"And furthermore," The Instructor continued after his pause, "you have changed the name of the heroine right in the middle of the story."

A few of the group members gave a start at this comment, but, recovering nicely, nodded their heads wisely as if they too had noticed this aberration. Ethan, however, was disconcerted. He had given up reading Miss Peavy's stories long ago, but now wished he had perused them, for he felt that he might have been the one to make this wise observation. Miss Peavy was not in the least troubled.

"This is easily remedied," she declared. "I have a 'find and replace' feature on my computer."

Next on the evening agenda was a poem which had been submitted by Mr. Hubert Longelly. As was their custom with poetry, the group read aloud. However, as sometimes happens when a group of people read aloud, the pace grew slower and slower as they covered page after page. Near the end of the fifth page, the pace had grown so slow that it seemed to come to a complete halt. The Instructor, with a snort, felt that the process had been completed, and, although there was a sixth and seventh page to go, called for a coffee break, saying that they would do the critique afterwards. Mr. Longelly's protests were drowned out by the scraping of chairs.

Ethan, by now having a full blown asthma attack from the effects of breathing Ms. Riley's Cinnamon Meadows, hurried to the men's washroom. Struggling for breath and supporting himself on the edge of the sink, he began to desperately fumble in his pant's pocket for his asthma inhaler. At that inopportune moment, Mr. Gibaharldimaxima strolled in. Quickly assessing Ethan's breathing difficulty, and his fumbling attempts to extract his inhaler from too tight jeans, he grinned with delight.

"Yah, yah, I know how it feels. Ms. Riley does that for me too," Mr. G. divulged. "But really, you should use a stall for your activity. I don't care, you know, but someone else might come in."

He disappeared into one of the stalls himself. Ethan, too distracted to catch Mr. G's meaning, continued to search his pant's pocket. Finally, he found the inhaler and took two hits. He felt better immediately, and with the attack now manageable, began to regulate his breathing. He conscientiously took long, slow breaths, attempting to empty his lungs completely with each exhalation, and fill his lungs with each inhalation.

"All done, eh." observed Mr. Gibaharldimaxima, emerging from his stall. "That was pretty quick for a man your age."

Ethan ignored him and concentrated on his breathing. He hated to miss any of the workshop, but knew that if he returned to sit beside Ms. Riley, his allergy to perfume would continue to plague him, so he made a decision to forgo the rest of the evening. He decided to return to the room before the rest of the participants, and privately, so as not to embarrass Ms. Riley, advise The Instructor of his difficulty, and insist that he must leave now in order not to exacerbate the problem. However, when he returned to the room, he discovered that The Instructor was having his fifteen-minute power nap. Head dropped back on the chair in what looked to be a most uncomfortable position, The Instructor was in full voice. Grey beard and mustache fluttered with each snore. Ethan, loathe to interrupt what looked like a much needed rest, seated himself to wait for the little snort that traditionally heralded the end of the power nap.

A wave of Cinnamon Meadows announced the return of Ms. Riley, and Ethan felt his eyes begin to itch and burn once more.

Mr. Gibaharldimaxima entered, looked greedily at the unoccupied chair next to Ms. Riley, but returned resignedly to his earlier seat next to Miss Peavy. Miss Peavy, undaunted by either previous critiques or The Instructor's loud snores, began to distribute the fourth chapter of her book. Mr. Gibaharldimaxima eagerly clutched the pages, and in order not to waste time, began to read immediately.

The rest of the workshop participants straggled in and respectfully awaited the little snort that would announce the beginning of round two. As time passed, Ethan began again to feel the full effects of Cinnamon Meadows.

Fifteen minutes stretched into twenty. Workshop participants looked at each other questioningly, and then, with one accord, looked to Mrs. Goodwind as the person who should break this deadlock. Mrs. Goodwind cleared her throat loudly, to no effect. At a loss for once, she began attentively to sort the papers in front of her. At last, The Instructor gave his little snort, and the second half of the workshop began. Unfortunately, Ethan's opportunity to speak privately with The Instructor was lost.

Mr. Longelly's poem was thoroughly critiqued. Several workshop participants commented that the poem seemed somehow unfinished. Unfortunately, in the ensuing discussion, Mr. Longelly's explanation that they had only read five of the seven pages was lost. The class proceeded to the next offering: a lengthy analysis of the benefits of a saving account versus the benefit of buying Canada Savings Bonds.

Fortunately for Ethan, the second half of the workshop was quite short, as about forty minutes had been taken up by The Instructor's power nap. As the group broke up, Ethan hurried from the room, groping once again for his inhaler. Mr. Gibaharldimaxima, in hot pursuit of Ms. Riley, and Miss Peavey, in turn pursuing Mr. Gibaharldimaxima, also made quick exits. Unfortunately, all four participants missed The Instructor's summary, as well as his complimentary remarks on how well the workshop had gone.

Daddy

I LOOK FOR MY SISTER by the school door, but she isn't there. Usually she just stands by the door after she eats. She says she's too old to play with the rest of us. She is older, fourteen, because she failed a grade, but I think she's just being a snot.

My best friend, Bonnie, called her a snob the other day, but I told Bonnie she's not a snob, and if she doesn't want to play with us, that's up to her.

I go round the corner and look through the window to see if I can see Mary in the room. And I do see her. Miss Bell is talking to her. Miss Bell is supposed to be the nicest teacher in the whole school, even if she is kind of fat, so I can't wait till I get to grade eight.

Miss Bell looks really interested in what Mary might have to say, but Mary, like always, isn't saying anything. Miss Bell reaches out to touch Mary's hand, but Mary yanks her hand away. She has on her "nothing" face, like she doesn't have any feelings at all, like she doesn't care for anybody or anything. Miss Bell takes her hand back, and both the teacher and my sister get up. Miss Bell looks at Mary as she leaves the room, and she has a kind of worried look on her face. I guess she thinks Mary is going to fail again. My sister pretends she doesn't care if she fails or not, but I know she does care. I don't know why she doesn't try harder and do her homework.

After school, when we are walking home, I ask Mary what the teacher wanted, and she says it's none of my business.

I don't bug her about it. I want to know really badly, but she'll just tell me I'm too little. That's what she says if she doesn't want to tell me anything, or if she doesn't want me to go somewhere with her, or if I want to keep the house key instead of her. I'm sick of hearing how I'm too little for this and too little for that. She thinks she's cool because she's older than me.

When we get home, I race up the stairs. I know if Mary gets to the TV first I'll never get to watch what I want. Sometimes, she changes the channel anyway when I'm watching, and when I get pissed off, she doesn't even care. That's what she does today. It's no use trying to change the channel back. Last time I did that, she called me some bad words.

I wish I was the oldest sister, but I would never treat any little sister like Mary treats me. I think she doesn't even like me, never mind love me. I miss my mom so much.

I don't want to watch Mary's show, so I get out my homework. I tell Mary she should do her homework too, but she pretends she doesn't hear me.

I would really like to have Bonnie or Melissa over, but my dad doesn't like for us to have friends over. He says that if my friends come here they'll make fun of us because we don't have any money, and he may be right. One time I heard Hanna laugh at my dress because it was way too big. It used to be my sister's dress. Hanna said, "Talk about reduce, reuse, recycle." I wanted to hit her, but I pretended to not hear her instead. But Bonnie and Melissa wouldn't laugh. I've seen Bonnie wear her older sister's dress, and I told her I really liked the embroidery on it. I don't, but she's my friend, and I didn't want her to feel like I felt when Hanna made fun of me.

When my dad comes home, I know he went and had a beer, because I can smell it. He says having a beer is good for his heart, and I know dad has a bad heart, so I don't care if he has a beer, except sometimes he falls down and gets sick. Usually he gets sick into the toilet, but sometimes he misses, and that is diiiisss-gusting.

Dad says he's tired, and he gives Mary some money and tells us to go out and get a pizza.

"Why can't I carry the money?" I ask.

"You're too little," Mary says.

After dinner, my sister and I watch TV. There's one show on at this time that both of us like. I squish into the corner so I'm not sitting on the broken spring.

"Mary," Daddy says. "You'd better come to my room to sleep tonight. I'm not feeling well."

Ever since my mom left, Mary has taken care of Dad when his heart acts up.

Well, I've had enough!

I jump up from the couch. "Let me come take care of you tonight, Dad" I say. "I'm big enough now."

Dad looks at me. I stand up really straight and stick out my chest. I know I'm growing up because I'm getting breasts now, even though I'm only eleven, and that's a sign I'm becoming a woman. And Mary told me about getting periods, and everything.

My dad looks at me. He looks really hard, and then he smiles, and suddenly I feel like hunching up my shoulders to hide my chest, but I don't do it. Mary says girls should be proud to become women.

"Yeah, you are getting big, Liz." he says. "I think you can come and take care of me tonight."

He goes into the kitchen.

But my sister whispers "Don't do it, Lizzie, let me do it."

It's been a long time since my sister called me Lizzie, so I look at her.

Mary is staring at the TV, but her face looks strange. Her chin is pulled into her neck and her eyes are squinched up.

Suddenly, my insides give a little jump, like they do when something scary happens real fast on TV, because my sister looks like she's going to cry. Then I think that's crazy, because I can't remember the last time Mary cried.

Wait a minute, I can remember. It was one morning after she took care of Daddy. I woke up, and she was crying. Right away, I figured Daddy had had a heart attack and died, but then I heard him grunting in the bedroom, so I ran in and he was okay. That happened about two years ago, just a little while after Mommy left us.

When I see my sister looking like she's going to cry, I get a little scared.

"How come you don't want me to do it?" I ask, but I know what she's going to say before she says it.

"You're too little, Lizzie." she says. "This time, you are too little."

But I know she's just mad because I'm finally getting to do some of the stuff she gets to do only because she's older than me.

"Too bad," I say. "I'm going to do it tonight."

I would stick out my tongue at her if I weren't getting grown up.

Inside, I feel strange, a little happy, a little scared.

Tonight, tonight I get to take care of my daddy.

The Beginning of the End

IT'S GOING TO BE A good day. It has to be a good day. This is the first day I've had off in a year and a half because of changing jobs. It's the first weekday when I don't have to jump up at 5 a.m., get Mikey out of bed, clean him up, and rush him off to day care. It's too much for a little kid, this getting up so early, being rushed through breakfast and into his clothes, and out into the cold.

And of course, my weekends are filled with laundry, cleaning, grocery shopping, cheque book balancing, and the other numerous household tasks.

I had set the clock for 5 a.m. for the sheer relief of being able to turn it off and go back to sleep. I know I would have woken up about five anyway. My body is used to that after all these years.

James goes out today, to *his* day care. I don't like that name for it, it makes an adult sound like a kid, but that's what the hospital calls it. Since his hospital stay after the last suicide attempt, it's been this day care, a way station on the road to recovery. And I sure hope he recovers quickly, because with my salary alone our finances are in poor shape. The fact is, we seem to be getting behind a little more each month, and I would love to stop counting pennies. It's been a long time since I bought toys or clothes for Mikey. And he's growing fast, his round belly showing below his undershirt.

Mikey wakes about six, and I pick him up and bring him back to bed with me. He snuggles down with his stuffed frog, and looks around, and eventually giggles and pokes me and his dad, giggles some more, stands up and looks out the window, then jumps on the bed.

"Mikey," I tell him, "we are going to have a great day today. We are not going to daycare. We are going to have a delicious breakfast, and then we're going to the park. We'll slide down the slide, swing on the swing, play in the sand. We'll read Pooh Bear, and Mommy will do the funny voices. We are going to have a scrumptious lunch. Then we'll have a nice nap, because you'll be tired by that time, and so will Mommy. And, then we will go swimming."

I pull up his pajama top and tickle his tummy, and he giggles some more. Then I pretend to bite his tummy, and he squeals and rolls around and laughs.

"For God's sake," James grumps, and I tell him it's after seven anyway, and he should probably be getting up. He's been sleeping more and more, not because he's doing anything. I still do all the cooking, and other housework, and take care of Mikey, but the doctors say all that sleeping is part of James being ill. For a minute I wish I had time to be sick too, but then I feel guilty about thinking that way. After all, he is my husband. Because I feel guilty, I tell him I'll make him a nice breakfast, and I do. I get up and cook pancakes and bacon for all of us. I don't have any maple syrup, so we make do with corn syrup. Mikey loves it, anyway.

James goes out around eight and leaves me the car so I can take Mikey swimming later.

Mikey and I get dressed. We are sitting on the couch talking about heading for the park, when the phone rings. It's James.

"Ruthie, help me," he says.

I don't know what to say. I don't know what this is about. He's supposed to be at the hospital.

"Help me, help me," he says.

"What? What's wrong?"

"I took all these pills."

"Where are you?"

"In the hospital."

"Tell someone, James. You're right there. There's doctors and nurses all around."

"I can't. I'm scared. I'm so scared. Help me, Ruthie, help me."

For another minute I try to get him to tell someone there, but he starts to cry and begs me again and again to help him.

I give up. I bundle Mikey into his coat and into the car. My hands are shaking, my insides are shaking. When I drop Mikey off at the day care, he looks at me in bewilderment. This isn't the park. Eileen takes one look at me and tells me to go on, that she'll get Mikey out of his coat. I look at Mikey's face and tears shoot into my eyes.

I drive to the hospital, my vision blurred by tears, the shakes taking over for a minute. Then I get hold of myself. I know I won't be of much use if I don't get control. Of course, I can't find a parking spot, and by the time I rush in the door I'm afraid it will be too late, but as I hurry down the hall someone from the day care stops me and tells me they got him. James is on a gurney in the hallway, looking disheveled and smelling of vomit. I'm told to ask him his name, my name, other questions, every 15 minutes to make sure he is alert. After a while, he tells me he had his stomach pumped. "Whew, I'll never do that again. I never want to get my stomach pumped again." He groans.

He feels sorry for himself.

In that second, a flash of rage hits me. I'm not sure why, and I don't stop to think about it.

For the next hour or so I ask him his name and other things he should be familiar with. After a while, he gets impatient. He tells me to stop asking. Then we have a consultation with the doctor. The bottom line is that they can't help him there anymore. He has to be admitted to a psychiatric hospital. Then the doctor asks me if I have any contacts in that hospital. I don't. Why would I? The doctor makes a lot of phone calls, makes arrangements. He is pretty sympathetic and gentle towards James, and tells me I have to support my husband.

A couple hours later, we are on our way. I am starving. I haven't eaten since breakfast.

As I drive, I take a look at James. He looks shabby, sways a little, and hangs his head down. I know I should feel sorry for him, but somehow I can't anymore.

When we get to the psychiatric hospital, there is another hour and a half of answering questions and admitting procedures. At first it looks like they don't want to admit him. Filled to overflowing already, I think. Eventually, we get James signed in, and I say words of comfort, and goodbye.

When I go to pick up Mikey, it's five o'clock already, and I am tired and even more starved. Eileen tells me Mikey's been acting out all day. He bit another kid, burst into tears because he couldn't have a toy he wanted, and generally was full of misery. I'd like to take him to McDonald's as a treat, but when I look in my wallet I just don't have the funds. At home I make us an omelet and toast. I don't have the energy for anything else. After I get Mikey to bed, I throw in a load of laundry and clean up a bit, but all the time there is something gnawing at me. I know I have to think about what happened today, but I stay busy instead.

I wake up about two in the morning. I know I have to get up in three hours, get Mikey to day care, and go to work. But, desperate as I am, I can't sleep. Anger is eating at me.

I get up and sit at the kitchen table, and all these thoughts swirl around in my mind. Why did this happen on my only day off? Did James do it deliberately? When will I have time for Mikey? Don't I count for anything? I know I have to support James, but who is going to support me? Do I want my son to grow up in this circus? Will James always be like this, with me always taking care of him? Don't I deserve some happiness in my life?

But the biggest question is this: If I think this through will it be an ending to my marriage?

I get up from the table and grab a pen and paper. I need to make a list, write down the good and the bad in this relationship. But even before I make the list, I know this is it. This is the beginning of the end.

Dream Wedding

I LOST MY HEAD AT the wedding.

I couldn't help it. First I lost my virginity to him, then I lost my leisure time doing his laundry and cleaning up after him, then I lost a good part of my bank account. My head was about all I had left.

It happened when they played that song "How could you give your love to someone else, and share your dreams with me". So I started thinking about the dreams he had shared with me. Erotic, he called them. I called them porn. To me, anything that involves groups or animals is porn.

His beloved, his bride, was my best friend Tiffany, and I, of course, was the maid of honour.

How Tiffany and I became such great friends, I'll never know. She was a little blonde, perky thing; I was a normal size. She was always laughing or crying; I was the calm one. He said she was ditzy. Turned out, he liked ditz. And little by little, he started to spend time with her. Pretty soon, I was history. A year later, when he came to tell me in person of their engagement, he had the nerve to suggest we be "friends with benefits". Hoping to fulfil one of his dreams, I guess.

Now, I was supposed to be laughing and clapping at his wedding. Certainly everyone else was laughing and clapping.

I did my congratulations speech. I started with platitudes about "dreams of a lifetime", and how "dreams really do come true". Before anyone figured it out, I slid in a few details of the groom's dreams. The silence was astounding. Thanks to my Toastmasters' training, I was able to take full advantage of that short silence and enlarged on a few more of his dreams.

There followed a short tussle with the best man, as he tried to wrench the microphone away. Then someone got smart and turned off the sound system. That's when I really lost my head and tried to make myself heard over the hubbub while being dragged out of the hall.

I lost a few friends when I lost my head, but still there was great satisfaction in knowing that the marriage was annulled by Tiffany's request, on the basis of non-consummation. Ha, I know for a fact that it was consummated *before* the wedding.

But tonight, I am going to dinner with the best man. He's not a dream man, he's a little chubby and starting to go bald, but in my real life, I've found my best man.

Conversations from the Rubble

FUCK! WHAT JUST HAPPENED HERE? One minute I'm scarfing back a cheeseburger, the next minute there's all this noise and screaming, now nothing. Ow! My fucking leg hurts. Hope it's not broken. I won't be winning the hurdles this year if that leg is broken. Shit, I won't even be competing. Something must have exploded here. How can something explode? It's a fucking mall, for fuck sake. This must be what it feels like to go into war. I never wanted that. Wow, it's dark in here. And quiet. Jesus, the place must have collapsed and I must be under it! Get me out of here!

***

My old bones are screaming. I'm pinned to the ground, and the ground isn't very comfortable. Something is sticking into my back, poking me, and I can't reach it. It feels like my arm is stuck to my side. It's black in here, no light at all. Oh Lord, I think the mall collapsed and I'm underneath. Is there anyone else in here with me? God, I don't want to die. I know I'm old, but I want to see my granddaughter one more time before I die. I'm going to pray to my God. God, please, just a few more years. I want to see Brianna grow up. I want to tell her of my hopes for her, how much I love her.

***

Oh my god, I think the building just collapsed. I don't believe it. Where's my cell phone? I'm going to call 911. I've got to get out of here and get back to that meeting. I haven't even had a chance to present the company's proposal to repair the mall. I know my cell is clipped to my belt, but I can't find it. It's like my hand can't feel anything. Shit, this isn't good at all. If I can just get my cell, and it's not broken, I can get help.

***

Fuck, my leg is killing me. It's so dark. I hate the dark. I don't care if I am eighteen; I still use a night light, although if anyone found out about that I would die of embarrassment. Christ, maybe I'm going to die anyway, and not of embarrassment. I got to keep this panic down. It's just dark, there aren't any bogey men. Is there anyone else in here with me? "Help," I scream. Well, I thought it was a scream, but I hardly made a sound. I scream again, and this time I hear someone else call out.

I call again, and a voice says, "Neil, Neil McIntosh, is that you?"

I'm so happy to hear a voice, I sob, but then I cover it up with a pretend cough. "Yeah," I say, "it's me."

"It's Isobel Weller," I hear. Shit, wouldn't you know it? Just yesterday I made fun of her wrinkles and her old lady's fat stomach. I told Jessica that if she ever gets fat like that, she's history, and I don't care if we're married or just hanging out together. Maybe Mrs. Weller didn't hear me make fun of her. Well, I guess she could probably figure out I was making fun of her. Now I'm trapped in here with her, and she probably hates me. She calls out to me asking if I'm hurt.

"Yeah, my leg is trapped, it may be broken," I say. Mrs. Weller tells me to just lie still, that when they find us they'll put the leg in a cast, that I'm young and the leg will heal. Yeah, well, what else can I do except lie still?

***

I had just started talking to God when I heard young Neil calling. Well, I guess God will understand. The boy is scared, and he's hurt, and it's more important that I offer him some comfort. So I ask him how he's doing, and try to reassure him. I want to get back to thinking about my granddaughter.

"Neil," I say, "Just give me a minute. I'm going to say a prayer to God."

I close my eyes and concentrate. I picture her, Brianna, smiling at me. Brianna, I think, this is your old grandma. Honey, I love you so much. Please, please finish school. Get the best grades you can. Education will help you with a good job. But, don't spend all your time on school, have some fun in your life. Choose your friends well and be a good friend. I know if I don't get out of here you're going to miss me, but I don't want you to sorrow too much. You're a young girl, be young, have fun. I know there's no such thing as telepathy, but I do this all the same. Sometimes Brianna tells me that she hears my voice in her head. I ask her what I say in her head, and she says that I tell her I love her, and she should do her math homework. Then I tell her that the first part of the message is more important than the second part, and we both laugh.

***

Crap, this has got to be the worst business trip of my career. First, a seven hour drive from Toronto, then my reservations mixed up, now I'm buried, and not just under work, either, ha, ha. And I found my cell phone, but it's smashed to pieces. How ironic that I'm answering the Request for Proposal to fix the roof, and the roof actually collapses. Okay, well, if I had my calculator with me, I could give them a new proposal around rebuilding. I wonder how much of the mall collapsed, if it was just a small section or the whole thing. If it's the whole thing, we'll need to do some hiring. That's good. That's a selling point. Jobs for the local's is always a good pitch. We'll bring in the experts, but that has a selling point as well; they'll need living quarters, and the local restaurants will do a good business. Yeah, I can make this an attractive offer. Let's see. I can do some of the work up without my calculator—I always did have a head for math. Okay, I might as well get started. At least, doing the calculations will keep my mind busy until I get rescued. I wonder if there is anyone else under here with me. There was an older lady at the next table, but I can't remember anyone else.

***

"Mrs. Weller," I say, and I hate the sound of my voice. I sound all weak and weepy like a little girl. I clear my throat and make it deeper.

"Sorry," I say. "Frog in my throat." Mrs. Weller says that she understands, there's a lot of dust in here.

"Shouldn't we be doing something to let people know we're down here, like yell or something? I mean, we just can't lie here and wait for people to figure it out." Mrs. Weller agrees with me, but she thinks yelling might be hard after a while and asks for any more suggestions. I bet ya she was a teacher when she was younger, asking for suggestions. I say maybe we could tap, and she agrees. I search around for something to tap with and find a rock or chunk of cement, and start a rhythmic tapping on the junk that's just above me. That loosens up dirt which falls in my face. Spitting and coughing, I move the tapping to a location more over my shoulder. I have plenty of room to move around, but I can't with my leg trapped like this.

***

I'm awful tired, God. I pray it is Your will that I get out of here alive. I don't want to be bedridden, or paralyzed, or anything like that either, but if that's the trade off, then I can make that trade-off, God. Or even if I die after they get me out of here. I just want to see Brianna again. I know if I die I'll be with Robert, and that will be a blessing, but please Lord, let me see my granddaughter again. I need to tell her how much I love her. My right arm is bent back, and I can't move it at all, but I lift my left arm and wipe the tears from my eyes. I can hear Neil tapping away, and after some listening I can tell he's tapping out a rhythm.

"That's really smart, tapping out a rhythm," I say. "The searchers will know it's not just something banging around and they'll know where to look for us."

It's the least I can offer the boy who's got to be scared out of his mind and is never going to admit it. I've heard other people say that Neil is a rotten egg, always in trouble, but what does that matter here and now? Lord, I'm tuckered out. I'm just going to try and relax for a minute.

***

Okay, I am good at math, but really, I guess I need more information. I still don't know how much of the mall collapsed, so I'm working with unknowns. Where are the search and rescue people anyway? Am I the only person under here? Earlier, I thought I heard some voices, but not now. Wait a minute, now I'm hearing some tapping. Finally someone is doing something. Probably be a couple hours though before anyone can get through. Shit, I'm thirsty. At least I'm in one piece. I can feel my foot is trapped, and it's kind of turned sideways, but just a sprain, I hope. Doesn't really hurt much. I hope it's not too much longer. First thing I'm going to ask for is a beer. And when I get back to TO I'm going to call up that brunette, what's her name? Jeanette, I think. Jeanette the brunette. I know I put that little piece of paper with her number in my wallet. She looked good, that woman. I'll see if she wants to get together for a drink. Maybe it's time to get serious with someone.

***

Mrs. Weller thinks I'm smart using a rhythm to the tapping. She'd freak if she knew I was doing that 'Shaggy'

song "It Wasn't Me". She probably hasn't had sex in like 30
years. Speaking of which, when I tell Jessica I almost died,
maybe she'll be more willing to put out. My arm's getting
pretty tired, though. In a few minutes, I'll ask Mrs. Weller to
tap for a while. I wonder how much time has passed? I wish
my mom was here. I don't mean here, trapped beneath the
mall, but just so I could talk to her. I was pretty mean this
morning. I'd like to tell her I was sorry. When I get out, I
mean, when we get out, I will tell her I was sorry. Well, she
will be angry with me for cutting classes, but not that angry,
seeing that I'm hurt and everything.

***

I don't want to be negative, but I start thinking about my
will. Now that I've got more to go around, I want to donate a
little something to my church. I just kept thinking about
making the appointment, and not doing it. This will teach me
to procrastinate. I guess I'm not too old to learn something.
My arm is really painful now. My shoulder feels like its' being
wrenched out of its socket, but I can't even move to try to
relieve it in any way. I'm just so tired; I think I'll close my
eyes for a bit.

***

God, I must have been in here for hours now. I've heard
some tapping, so I yelled, but I didn't get any reply. I'm
beginning to think the tapping is in here with me. Every time
I put out a hand I can feel a kind of cave around me. I guess
that's why I'm still alive, I'm in some kind of cave made by
falling girders or something. When are they going to get me
out? Do they even know I'm in here? They must. They would
try to account for everyone and I'm sure I'll be reported
missing when I don't get back to the meeting. Relax Jack, I
tell myself, this is just going to take time.

***

Fuck, I can't feel anything from my leg anymore. Is that a good sign or a bad sign? I'd like to ask Mrs. Weller, but I think she's sleeping or something. After I tapped for a while she tapped out "Happy Birthday" a bunch of times. Wouldn't you know an old lady would tap out a song like that? At least it wasn't "Rock of Ages", or something religious. I don't know how long I've been in here but I'm really thirsty now, and hungry too. I think I slept or passed out or something for a while. Mom must be wondering where I am by now. School must be over and maybe Jessica told her I cut classes, and she'll be calling around trying to find me. Shit, it's so dark in here. What if there's a rat or something in here? I don't care about mice, but what if there's a rat in here? It will bite me if it feels trapped. I think I hear something. "Mrs. Weller, Mrs. Weller," I yell.

***

I wake up because I hear someone calling my name, and for a second only I think it's Brianna, then I remember I'm trapped underneath the mall. It's that boy, Neil, calling me.

"I'm here, Neil," I call back. He tells me he just wants to know if I'm okay. He's petrified, I know. I want to talk to him but I can't think of anything to say. What do I have in common with a teenage boy? Then something comes to me.

"Do you know what your name means, Neil?" I ask him. I only know because when Robert and I named our own two boys, Neil was a name I favoured. Robert didn't favour it, so we compromised on names we both liked.

"Neil means champion," I tell the boy. "And you, Neil, are a champion. You are. You're in this terrible situation with me, and you're coming up with suggestions to help us, and you're trying to make sure I'm okay. You're a true champion." I think I hear Neil sob, but I could be mistaken.

***

I'm so thirsty I can't stand it. I think I've been sleeping on and off, but I'm not sure. I guess things are kind of bad now. Shit, if only we had got to fix that roof, I wouldn't be here now. I don't know why I'm finding it so hard to breathe. I thought at first there was something sitting on my chest, but when I went to push it off there was nothing there. I think I did sleep, because for a while I thought I was back in TO, safe in my own bed.

***

God, what's happening? I thought I saw my mom, but I was either sleeping or hallucinating, I don't know what. I wish I could talk to her though. I thought Mrs. Weller was supposed to be tapping now, but she's not. Maybe she's asleep. I'm not going to wake her up, she's an old lady and she probably needs a lot of sleep. Boy, I'm actually pretty tired too, but I'm going to tap a bit anyway.

***

Jesus, what is this pain in my chest! If only I had some water.

***

Fuck, I must have slept. It's Mrs. Weller's turn to tap for a while. Mrs. Weller, Mrs. Weller. Jeeze, how can she sleep like that when it looks like we're going to die? Oh, fuck! Mrs. Weller, Mrs. Weller. Oh, god I wish I could talk to my mom.

You Can Never Be Too Rich Or Too Thin

TODAY, I MUST GO SEE my sister. Today, I must decide. Open or closed?

This is what happens. The organs shrink. Fluid and electrolytes are out of balance. Fatigue is ever present. Dizziness occurs. Stomach hurts. Bloating. Constipation. Muscles disappear. Bone density shrinks. Menses stops. Memory fails. Kidneys fail. Heartbeat is irregular. Cardiac arrest.

When did it begin? I don't know. I think it is almost impossible to tell.

One day, I was seeing my little sister, a young teen. She was a little chunky, yes, and this is what we were all used to seeing. Then, next time I noticed her, she suddenly had some curves. "Felicity, look at you," I said. "You're growing in to a young woman. Look at all those curves." She blushed. Felicity has always been a little shy.

Did it start then, when she saw she was getting breasts? Did she decide she didn't want breasts? Did boys and men looking at her breasts bother her?

We went on to talk about school. She was starting grade nine that year, and was looking forward to joining different activities. Felicity has always been a joiner. When she moved out of junior school into middle school, she was really nervous about making friends. I, with my six year advantage, advised her to join everything she was interested in, and if she wasn't interested in anything, join something anyway. It was the way to make new friends. Felicity was planning on playing a musical instrument, joining the track and field, and the chess club.

"A well rounded program," I said.

I was proud of her. She was, of course, on the honour roll. Felicity had always been a good student, not only getting good grades, but volunteering for whatever good works the school was involved in. She had won the citizenship award in grade eight.

Felicity was living with me by the time she went into grade ten. Mom had passed away with cancer when she was four and I was ten, and Dad had done a great job raising us. But eventually he had remarried. Felicity and Maria, my dad's new wife, didn't get along. I couldn't find any fault with Maria, except she was from a different culture and stricter than either my sister or I were used to.

Dad was great, though. He gave me more than sufficient funds to cover Felicity's basic expenses and gave Felicity a generous allowance. My job was decently paid, and I didn't need any financial help for myself, but I couldn't have supported Felicity too. But with Dad's help, we were pretty comfortable. Plus, we were frequently to dinner at Dad's place, and Maria was an excellent cook. Nobody disagreed about that.

I had boyfriends on and off, but nothing serious, and thanks to Dad, we had a two bedroom apartment, so I didn't feel put upon for privacy or any other reason. And when I didn't have a Friday night date, Felicity and I would cuddle up on the sofa and watch some old, soapy movies, or TV re-runs. The Brady Bunch was a favourite for both of us for some reason. It appeared a good solution to the step mother/step daughter dilemma had been found.

Around mid-winter that year I begin to wonder why Felicity was running every morning. Surely, track and field was over. But when I asked, Felicity said that track and field was coming in the spring, and she was getting a jump on the start of the season.

Maria began to get irritating that winter. She was always encouraging us to eat, eat, eat. I pointed out that I was eating, eating, eating. One day, I was helping with the dishes when she expressed her concerns. "That Felicity, she's too skinny," she said. I looked at Maria, who was "pleasingly plump" when she married my dad, but was now becoming unpleasingly plump. I didn't need to voice my thoughts; I could see that Maria got my point. Nevertheless, she still insisted, "She's too skinny."

That summer, Felicity continued to run every day. I noticed that her once luxurious hair was getting dry, and I advised her to stay out of the sun more, or use a hat, and I got her a good conditioner. Her skin looked a little yellow also, and I teased her about using a rub on tan to impress the boys. But one day, I saw her in a bikini, and I was startled at how thin she was. That evening, I sat her down, and we had a good talk about taking care of herself, and about eating healthy. She still ate popcorn on Friday evenings, but I noticed she didn't put melted butter on it anymore.

Felicity had her first boyfriend that summer, and although I was pretty sure she wasn't sexually active, like most 15 year olds, she was obsessed with having a good figure.

And I had met a man, Thomas, that summer. It was a good relationship, and now that Felicity was old enough to be home by herself, I spent weekends at Thomas' place. He and Felicity got on well enough, although a couple times Thomas asked me whether Felicity's health was okay.

At Thanksgiving dinner that October, all hell broke loose. Dad had been concerned about Felicity's teeth, and was demanding that she go to the dentist. Felicity was claiming there was nothing wrong with her teeth, although it was plain that she had some cavities. We all knew she had a fear of the dentist. On top of that, Maria had been going on again, insisting that my baby sister eat more. So Felicity did.

At the end of the dinner I went into the kitchen under the pretext of helping Maria with the dishes. I was thoroughly pissed off by this time and I started whisper-yelling at her to lay off, leave Felicity alone. To my utter amazement Maria burst into tears.

"Listen," she said. I listened, but Maria didn't say anything more. I was about to start my tirade again when I heard it. Felicity was in the bathroom, vomiting.

"You and your dad, you wouldn't listen," Maria said.

And she was right. We should have been listening, and we should have been looking.

This is what the person on the outside sees. Thin, thin, thin, hidden under baggy clothes. Dry, thinning hair. Yellow, sagging skin. Knobby joints. Brittle nails. Reddened eyes. Decayed teeth. Cold hands. No breasts. No hips. Fine hair all over the body.

This is what the person, while still alive, looking out, sees. Fat. Fat, fat, fat.

Dad and I together confronted Felicity. She already knew there was a problem.

The next five years were a roller coaster of hope and hell. A counselor, hospital visits, regular weigh-ins, a nutritionist, support groups for both Felicity and myself, a residential treatment program. Dad retired and devoted more time to his daughter. Thomas disappeared under the constant pressure.

There were some weight gains, some lessening of the compulsive running, some recognition by Felicity that there was more to this than feeling fat.

But at the end of it, Felicity died. She died at the ripe old age of 21. And she did look old, extraordinarily so.

And today I must decide on the coffin. Open or closed?

Oh, That's Why

I CAN HEAR THEM OUT there, their voices soft in the soft evening. Occasionally there is some muted laughter, sometimes louder laughter, then a little conversation.

I'm glad. Frequently I don't know where Trevor is—out at the mall, driving the streets with Kenny in his old car, getting drunk? I don't know. That's why I'm glad they've taken to spending some evenings in my backyard. There are six of them out there now, 17 and 18 year olds, lounging around on the plastic lawn chairs and picnic table.

I wonder what they talk about. Girls, probably, teachers, grades, girls, prom night, girls, parents, cars, and of course, girls.

I need to put in some laundry, and I know I left my sweater out there this afternoon. I open the back door, and a small pool of light spills out. The boys are near the back of the yard, in a semicircle. Something about their seating arrangement bothers me, but I don't know why.

"What do ya want, Ma?" Trevor says, as if I have no right to come into my own back yard. Oh well, at least they're here and not getting into trouble.

I tell Trevor I want my sweater, and Kurt says, "No worries, Mrs. B., I got it." He jogs to the back door with my sweater. I hope Trevor is that polite when he is at his friends' parents.

I put the laundry in, watch a little TV, fold the laundry, play on the computer, empty the dishwasher, and make my lunch for the following day. When I take the garbage out, I exchange a few words about the weather with the man bringing out the garbage from the small apartment building two doors down. By now it's about 10 o'clock, and I wish they would all go. I don't want to disturb them, though, for I would prefer Trevor be here then out some place. Finally, they do leave, at about 11p.m., and Trevor goes up to bed after wishing me a good night.

I'm in my night clothes when I notice that one of the boys has left his jacket draped over a chair. It looks like leather, and I decide to go out and bring it inside for safe keeping.

I look at the semicircle of chairs. Now I figure out what was bothering me earlier. They are all turned slightly to the left, instead of facing each other. I pick up the jacket, and when I turn, I see it. It's a large screen, wall mounted television, second floor in the small duplex two doors down, and clearly visible. And what's playing on it doesn't need any explanation, plot or dialogue. And now I know why these boys are gathered in my back yard. It's free porn.

Home Invasion

IT ALL STARTED WITH ONE little mouse.

Well, it was probably two little mice, but I only saw one of them. I was sitting on a footstool talking to my boss on the telephone. I was home ill, the drapes were closed, and the room gloomy, when I saw something drop out of my African Violet. I knew immediately. It was not a leaf. A leaf doesn't stretch out and land on tiny feet. With tremendous willpower, I refrained from screaming and dropping the phone. I didn't want my boss dialing emergency services and reporting some kind of home invasion at my address. I remained calm and pulled my feet up. It's a well-known, though not a well-documented, fact that mice run up women's legs. Why they don't run up men's legs, I don't know.

After my call to my boss ended, I pulled some clothes on my fever-racked body, applied some mascara, and headed off to Canadian Tire to get bait. I put the bait out, it got eaten, I put more bait out, it got eaten, I put more bait out and, hallelujah, it was not disturbed.

I was the winner.

So I thought.

Several weeks later, I started the Christmas baking. It was obvious the mice had already had Christmas dinner, and many more dinners, in the top cupboard where the flour was kept. Mice do not have good toilet manners. I had to throw out anything that wasn't in a metal container. I also had to throw up several times.

Then there was the nasty job of cleaning the shelf. That took several rolls of paper towels and industrial strength cleaner. As I stood on the kitchen step ladder I knew that if a mouse appeared I would need to perform an amazing athletic feat: I would need to leap off the top step of the ladder, avoid contact with the walls, and land safely at least six feet away. Fortunately, I was not forced to display my athletic prowess.

Once I had cleaned the shelf I got on with the baking. With the cookie dough prepared, I reached into the bottom cupboard for the cookie pans. A mouse scurried past my hastily withdrawn hand. I leapt three feet into the air, giving the rodent ample time to run underneath me and disappear under the fridge. Of course, the fridge was to be my next destination. I needed eggs.

Late that night, I woke up thinking with dread about the open house I was having. Would I have enough chairs? I had invited 15 friends—would they still be friends after an encounter with Mickey and Minnie? After much calculation, I decided that, if there was an appearance, I would have enough furniture for guests to jump on as long as I had no more than 12 people at one time. As there were several men invited, I wouldn't need furniture for them to leap on. Being full of testosterone they have to claim they aren't afraid of anything, never mind a mouse.

It was on Boxing Day that I really became aware of the extent of the rodent problem. I was cleaning out all the cupboards. (Whoever says house cleaning isn't exciting hasn't tried to clean out the cupboards under the sink while standing on a kitchen chair). Mice kept popping out of the cupboards, heating vents, and woodwork. After a while, seeking relief, I retreated to the living room. Outlined against the deflector over the hot air register were two mice. I began to feel like I was in some low budget horror movie – 'Mouse-o-phobia,' maybe.

The next day I began my search for the ultimate exterminator.

After several phone interviews, I reached Brian. "You need to find the source," he told me on the phone. This was something I had not even thought of. He said he could come the next day at 6:30 p.m. I immediately felt better.

As I walked into my home after work the next day, a fat (or pregnant) mouse jogged across the floor. I'd had enough.

I retreated to my bedroom, packed a suitcase with clothes for the next day, and sat with my feet up on the bed waiting for Brian. At 6:40, the telephone rang. My heart sank as I snatched up the receiver. I was sure it was Brian and he was going to say he couldn't come that evening.

"I was a little delayed. I'll be there in ten minutes," he said.

I ran to stand in my well-lit front door and wait for my hero. Juliet could not have longed for her Romeo any more than I longed for Brian.

Brian was as reassuring in person as he had been on the phone. Tromping around in his big boots, he kept up a continuous chatter about rodent habits and reassured me that soon all would be well. He peered into all the heating vents, the cupboards, the nooks and crannies, and climbed his ladder to look into the attic.

"Here's the source," he exclaimed from the top of the ladder, his voice resonating inside the attic. He tossed in about 50 packages of bait.

"It's vitamin D," he said.

"Wait a minute," I protested. "Vitamin D! I'm not trying to grow bigger and better mice."

"It gives them a heart attack," Brian explained.

I followed my hero around the house babbling my appreciation. Kindly, he told me a story of receiving a panicky phone call at 3 a.m., and arriving to find a six-foot tall, 200 pound man with a broom in his hand, cowering in one corner of his living room, and a tiny mouse cowering in the other corner. It was a story that made me feel better.

"Seven to ten days, and remember, you're bigger than they are," he said, going out the door. It was amazing. That was exactly what my mother used to say to my sister when she became hysterical about spiders. I rushed up the stairs, got my suitcase, and made my way to the nearest decent motel.

The next day, I had gained sufficient strength from my hiatus to return home. The mouse sightings continued, but now they didn't even need to be disturbed to put in an appearance. They appeared singly and in groups, and barely retreated when I yelled at them and stamped on the floor.

They sat in the wall heating vents, their tails hanging out; they ran across the middle of the kitchen floor while I ate dinner; they ran into the bathroom so that I couldn't use the facilities before I went to my restless sleep. They danced the fandango in the dining room. Or maybe it was the salsa. It didn't bother them when I turned off the radio. They continued to dance, as if to a different drummer. The boy mice wore bow ties; the girl mice wore tiaras, and did pirouettes. They absolutely didn't look like they were dying; they were having a great time.

I was not.

The mice seemed to be getting bigger and healthier than before. Their fur was glossier, their eyes shinier; they were plumper.

I called Brian. He came again, checked the bait and replaced packages. He listened while I described the erratic rodent behavior. I didn't mention that they were dancing the fandango in formal attire. I didn't want Brian to know that he had a neurotic woman dealing with psychotic mice.

He reassured me that the bait made the rodents act strange before it killed them, so we knew they were taking it. I still didn't mention the dancing.

In the meantime I went nowhere inside my home without turning on lights. I groped blindly around corners to hit the switch before stepping into a room. Where the light was at the other end of the room, I used a flashlight. I'm surprised that my neighbours didn't call the police to report a burglar creeping around my house. I placed kitchen chairs at strategic locations so I would have something solid to leap up on at any appearance. One night when I was talking to a friend on the phone she asked me to get her an address.

"I can't," I said. "I can't get off this chair, there's a mouse running around the floor."

"Get a broom and chase it away," she said.

"Okay," I quietly hung up the phone, curling up on the chair.

After a week I decided to act in a more courageous manner. Several mice were sitting in the wall heating vent with their tails hanging out. I decided to use the broom to knock them down the heating vent into the furnace.

I picked up the broom and started to advance upon them. What a triumph this would be! This was the day when I first became aware of the true meaning of the word "ambivalence". Fear of the mice kept me from advancing upon them. I can't even say it was two steps forward, and one back. It was really half a step forwards, and a step backwards, followed by a dead stop. Victory was theirs.

For the next few weeks I did everything to avoid going home. I worked long hours. I ate out. I accepted social invitations to join people I didn't like. My social life improved; my home life did not. Finally, I moved temporarily to the hotel room.

When my Christmas tree became a fire hazard, I gritted my teeth and risked going back. Removing the decorations and putting the tree outside became a workout that combined ballet and martial arts.

The hotel bills ate away at my bank accounts.

I visited my home most evenings, peering in the windows, looking for live or dead rodents. Most evenings I didn't have the courage to go inside. Eventually, the dancers ceased dancing, the joggers ceased jogging, and I saw neither live nor dead mice when I peered in the windows.

I called Brian to do an inspection. He declared the house rodent free. After approximately three endless weeks and a lightened bank account, this sad and traumatic affair had come to an end.

Brian is still my hero.

Gone

IT'S GETTING COLDER, AND SOMETHING in me says that I won't find her here, but my mind knows that's just the cold talking. So I keep on.

So many young girls, mini-skirts, thigh-high boots, fishnet stockings, blouses opened to expose their breasts. They must be freezing. Green, blue and orange hair. And some normal colours. A few smoking, though not as many as I expected. I guess the health message reaches even here.

I am looking for the small upturned nose, the fine light brown hair, the big blue eyes. Then I put the hair out of my mind. Hair can be dyed, as I see in front of me. I scan the faces. I am met with blank, curious or indifferent looks. Mostly indifferent.

About half a block ahead of me, a girl bends into the window of a car, laughing and chatting. As she straightens slightly, I see her profile. Smooth, pale skin, a snub nose, large blue eyes rimmed in black.

Could be, could be.

The girl puts her head back into the car window, negotiating. I start to hurry, going as fast as my arthritic knee will let me.

"Melly, Melly," I call, and grab her by the upper arm. Startled, the girl pulls out of the car window, hitting her head against the rim. The car jumps ahead, the driver spooked.

"Melly," I say again. The girl glares at me

"What the fuck are you doing?" she says. "I was almost done for the day."

It isn't Melanie's voice, not as I remember it. But then, it was so long ago. And she was a little girl. How could my memory be that accurate?

"You stupid, ugly old bitch" she says, and gives me a shove. I stagger and land on my right hip. The pain is bad. The girl starts to walk away. After a few steps, she returns.

"Old bitch," she says again, and kicks me in the leg, though not too hard. She walks away again.

Tears are in my eyes, and I start to get up. I'm having a hard time with it, and I decide to wait for a few minutes before trying again, although it's so cold on the ground. I think of homeless people while I wait. I think of how they have to endure the cold day after day, and worse, night after night. I pray she isn't homeless.

I decide to try again when a car pulls up beside me. It is white, with blue and red., A large police officer gets out.

"Just a minute, Ma'am." he says, and goes behind me, lifts me, and helps me to the back seat of the car. He gets back in on the driver's side, turns on the heat. He and his partner turn to look at me.

"Ma'am," he says, "what are you doing in this area?"

The pain in my knee and hip is killing me, and I don't reply. The large officer gives me a short lecture on safety, asks me what happened. I tell them I fell. I pass over my identification when they ask, and then wait as they call in. I've been through this before. The officer turns to look at me, not unkindly.

"Come on, grandma, I'll give you a ride to the subway," he says. I shoot him a look. He turns a little pink. "Sorry Ma'am," he says, "I didn't mean no disrespect."

"Any disrespect." I correct him. "My car is just around the corner about a block down."

"Yes, Ma'am," he says, and starts the police car. In the rearview mirror I see the other officer give him a smirk.

My knee and hip stiffen as I drive home, and I'm careful not to slip as I make my way down my own sidewalk. I know I should put ice on my hip to stop it swelling, but I can't stand the thought of any more cold. I put my gel bag to heat in the microwave instead, and sit there and think. I smile to myself a bit as I remember the young officer. Maybe I shouldn't have been so hard on him. After all, he was only trying to help.

I get up and hobble to the spare bedroom. I look at all the gifts. I've arranged them chronologically. The paper on the older ones is beginning to fade.

The oldest is the rag doll I got her for her fourth Christmas. It has red yarn hair, a denim dress, and a red pinafore over the dress. I had it made for her. She would have loved it. Beside it sits a smaller gift with balloons and teddy bears on the wrap. That would have been for her fifth birthday. She would have just started school, half-days in kindergarten, and I carefully picked out several books, brightly coloured, some of them stories of children who were just starting school, making friends, and getting used to the teacher. The next package, Christmas again, contained a blue velvet dress with a wide sash. Just the thing for a five-year old girl. My son used to complain laughingly that I bought his daughter only blue clothes, but I knew that he loved those big blue eyes as I did.

As time went on, I found it more difficult to pick out the gifts. What would a fourteen year old girl like? Would she be a tomboy and want sports shoes, or would she prefer clothes? I looked at the girls in the neighbourhood. Would she be like those girls? Would she want her eyebrow pierced for her birthday?

Now she's nineteen, and the choices are even more difficult. Would she be thinking of getting married? Would she be in university and want something practical? This year's gift would need a lot of thought.

First things first.

I hobble back to the kitchen, pull the warm gel bag out of the microwave, press it against my hip and sink into a kitchen chair.

I pull my notebooks to me and review and think. I look at the old pictures; I look at the computer enhancement. Time to get another of those. She's about fifteen in the last one. The police won't help with that any more, and even the missing children's support group, compassionate as they are, think this is a lost cause.

I think of how she loved going to kindergym when she was three. Maybe that's a part of her that survived. I know it's not probable, but maybe she was taken care of, maybe whoever it was only wanted a child of their own. I have to think of all the possible options. A health club is another place to look.

I write "health club" under *Possibilities*. I pull the yellow pages towards me and start a list. Tomorrow, I will start on the health clubs.

Maybe. Maybe this time.

Conversation For One

OH, MISS, THANKS SO MUCH for bringing dinner. Turkey today? I love turkey. Pardon? What did you say? Do I really? Well, I do love all the meals you bring.

Miss, look at this lovely teacup. I got it from my mother, who got it as a wedding gift. That was, oh, a long, long time ago.

Wait, Miss, you don't have to go yet, do you? This teacup was hand painted; see the roses. They're kind of faded now. I remember they were much redder before, when my mother first gave it to me. Would you believe, I still miss my mother. I always said that I would leave this teacup to my daughter, but I never had a daughter, and my sons, well, they just don't care. They're busy with their jobs and their families, I guess.

Oh, just one more minute, Miss. Would you like a cup of tea? No? Well, do have a biscuit, please. Not allowed to? Why ever not? I know, I know, all you young people are in such a rush. Not young? Of course, you are. I understand, someone else is waiting, and you don't want the meals to get cold. Maybe you can come back another time and we can visit. Well, I guess you're busy, don't have much time. Time is all I have. Well, my niece did say she would come visit next month. Bye, then.

Oh, is that the mailman? Hello, hello, Mr. Wilson. Anything for me? Well, can I give you a nice cup of tea, then? I'm sure you can use it after all that walking.

Josh

THE DAY IS WARM AND dry, giving way to a cool, dry evening. Allison stretches and yawns comfortably as she walks toward her car. It had been a perfect day, a perfect time, to practice her tennis serve, and doubly welcome after the wet weather they have had the rest of the week. She is glad she smeared on the sunscreen, otherwise she would probably be burned by now. The mid-October leaves have begun to change colour, but are not yet red and orange. Instead they are a pale green and yellow, and the sunlight that filters through has a mellow golden look. Allison decides that there will be a great sunset, for how else could such a day end?

She needs to sort her tennis balls; there was a puddle of water where she was practicing, and some of the balls are wet. She will drop the damp balls on a piece of cardboard in the trunk of her car. The dry tennis balls she'll leave in the basket.

Allison is just opening the car door when someone speaks to her. A young man, or boy, is standing on the sidewalk asking a question. Allison can not hear what he is saying, so she shuts the car door and walks toward him with her tennis racquet still in hand. The boy—or young man, for Allison can never decide at what age boys become young men—is about nineteen, maybe twenty years old. He is dressed in army fatigues, or some kind of combat camouflage, and he is carrying a large duffel bag. Allison wonders if he is an army recruit. She's sure there isn't any army camp near here. An uneasy feeling bothers the edges of her mind. She knows there is something incongruent here.

As they draw closer, the boy speaks again, with a strong French accent. Allison pauses before she understands that he is asking how to get to Islington Avenue and Highway 401. He has a hand drawn map showing Islington Ave. and the

401 intersecting. As she pushes back her long, pale brown hair, and looks at the map, a second boy walks into the parking lot. This young man is about 18 years old, and has bad acne. He is dressed in the same manner as the first boy.

It's then that Allison registers what seems incongruent. Neither boy has the short hair required by the army. Both have "mohawks", that strip of long hair down the centre of the head with the sides shaved bald. However, both boys are allowing the shaved area to grow out, and it is now several inches long, making the long centre hair less noticeable.

The second boy sits down on the curb that borders the grassy area and the parking lot. He puts his elbows on his knees and his head in his hands. He stares at the ground.

The boy she is talking to tells her that they are hitch-hiking to Montreal tonight. Allison explains to the boy that they have been walking south on Islington Avenue, away from the 401. It is a long walk to the 401, and Allison doubts that anyone will give them a ride. The boy she is talking to turns to speak French to the younger boy. "Henri," he says, and Allison overhears the words "401" and "Islington". She knows he is telling Henri that they have been walking in the wrong direction. Henri stares out in front and drops his head into his hands again.

Allison is concerned about both boys, but particularly about the younger boy. He is the most discouraged looking kid that she has seen in a while. She tells the boys that it isn't very safe for them to be standing out on a highway at night. She attempts to persuade the boys to stay in a youth hostel, and go on to Montreal in the morning. The boy she is talking to smiles at her condescendingly and states that they will go to Montreal tonight. The younger boy looks at the ground.

Allison suggests to the boys that they take the bus to the subway, and the next bus north to the 401. The boy tells her that they have no money. Allison looks at the boy sitting on the curb and wonders whether they honestly have no money, or whether they are conning her. She thinks of her own son, and decides that she would prefer to lose the money to a con than have the two boys stuck without any money. She can get to a bank machine first thing in the morning. She goes to her car and her purse, and comes back with a couple of loonies and a five dollar bill. The two boys are genuinely surprised at her giving them money, and are sincere in their thanks. Allison is glad she gave them the help. She points out the bus stop to the boys; it is only about 20 feet away. She returns to her car feeling good about the decision.

A few minutes later, Allison has finished sorting the tennis balls. The boys are still at the bus stop, sitting on their duffel bags. And just past them, Allison sees Josh coming to find her. Allison smiles to herself, watching Josh's loose unselfconscious walk. His elbows sticks out, his hands looks too big for his arms, and his knees are huge and boney under the stylish baggy shorts. His feet are clown feet. At fourteen, Josh has inherited his father's height and dark skin, but not yet his muscular build.

The swim team try-outs had taken place earlier today, and by the pleased look on Josh's face, she knows he has made the team. Spotting her, he lifts his arm, waves, and yells, "Hi, Maw", just as if he had been born and brought up in the country rather than as a city kid. A big grin lights up his face. Allison wears a matching grin.

Josh will pass by the two boys at the bus stop, and Allison hopes they won't ask him for money. Josh – healer of hurt birds, peacemaker, funny-faced clown to crying babies – will cheerfully dig in his pocket and give them whatever change he has left from his paper route collection. Josh will figure that they need it more than he does, and he will give it. The boys stand up as Josh draws close to the bus stop.

Then it happens.

The older boy reaches out and shoves Josh on the shoulder. It is one of those short, sharp shoves that men use to challenge or goad each other. And Allison hears, "Get out of my way, nigger." She is stuck to the sidewalk.

But, I just helped them.

The younger boy giggles. The first boy shoves Josh again, this time with both hands. Josh stumbles and falls backwards onto the street.

Horns blare, brakes screech and a small red car swerves into the other lane and comes to a stop.

"What's your problem, nigger?" smirks one of the boys.

Allison is running.

The door of the small red car opens, and a very large, black man gets out. He's wearing a T-shirt with the words POWERHOUSE GYM inscribed on the front.

The two boys take one look at him, mutter "Jezuss", pick up their duffel bags, and flee across the park.

When Allison reaches Josh, he is scrambling to his feet. She reaches out a hand to help, but he jerks away from her. Tears fall from his eyes, snot runs from his nose. On his face is hurt, rage, and shame. He turns his back to her and walks away, not bothering to brush himself off.

Allison stares after him. Her gut churns.

The sun is setting; the mellow, golden look is gone from the day.

The Visit

I VISIT MY MOTHER AT Sunset Acres.

My son comes with me. We have always lived far away from my family; the twice yearly visit not enough for him to forge a strong bond with his grandmother. Yet, in his early 20's, he comes with me out of a sense that family is important.

My mother is propped up in bed, looking small and tired. A short, once sturdy woman, she laments what little weight she now carries has followed gravity's demands and settled in her hips.

This is the woman who raised five daughters. This is the woman who cared for us through childhood illnesses, comforted us after the cruelties of best friends, and saved us from things that went bump in the night. When we heard unexplained noises around our old, isolated farmhouse, she would pick up the baseball bat and say, "Lock the door after me girls, and don't open it again until you hear my voice."

We would hear her circling around the house, calling to potential intruders in her strong, fearless voice, "Come out now, come on." Then her voice would be at the back door. When we let her back in, she would say "There's nothing to worry about girls. Go to bed now." And we would return to bed, forever safe.

My mother is wearing a pink bed-jacket of some shiny material.

"Do you want this on, Ma?" I ask, and she shakes her head. We wrestle her out of it and into her old grey sweater. She immediately looks more comfortable.

I have asked my mother to help me learn French. French is her first language; English is the language she learned in her early 30's. I failed French in grade 9, dropped out of it in grade 10. Now, in middle age, I am trying again, and have enrolled in a beginner's course in conversational French.

I ask my mother to say simple phrases to me in French so that I can repeat and translate. Then I try to say simple phrases to her in French. We do this for a while, then, suddenly, we are out of words. Strangely, neither of us can recall any more common, everyday phrases. We sit and think.

My mother says something in French, but I am thinking too hard and don't catch what she says. I look up at her. Her hand is over her mouth, and behind her hand she is smiling.

"What?" I say. "What did you say to me?"

She takes her hand away from her mouth.

"Fermer tu," she says.

"Did you hear that?" I ask my son, "Your grandmother just told me to shut up."

He shakes his head, bewildered, not knowing how to react.

My mother and I explode into laughter. Shoulders shaking, we lean forward and look gleefully into each other's contorted faces.

Our hearts rise, meet, and touch once more.

The Drive

"GOODBYE JIMMIE" SAM SAYS TO himself as he files out of the chapel behind the first rows. He knows what Jimmie would say, if he could say anything now: "You won't be far behind me, boy-o." It had been almost a password between them. After Jimmie's first grope, first big drunk, first anything, he would say to Sam, "You won't be far behind me, boy-o," and then he would laugh his big laugh. He was usually right.

Not this time, Jimmie. Not this time.

Sam smooths his hand over his grey hair, and pulls the front of his jacket across the mustard stain on his white shirt. He was sure this suit had fit him better last time he wore it.

He makes his way slowly to the car, shaking hands as he goes, and he thinks about the good times. He thinks of how he and Jimmie had laughed at each other's army issue haircuts, and of their first visit to a whorehouse, both of them panicky, but neither of them admitting it; and of how they had both got drunk at their own and the other's wedding. He thinks about how Jimmie moved to the country after Susan was born, and of how they still knew each other's thoughts on the rare times they got together.

Sam pulls the Monte Carlo into the line-up for the procession to the cemetery. He knows they're going to Ogden. It's where Marjorie had been put to rest, next to her parents. It's what Marjorie had wanted, and Jimmie had been fine with that, even though there had been a cemetery closer to their own community.

Sam doesn't know where Ogden is. In the church, when the minister was giving directions to the graveyard, he was thinking again about Jimmie, about how they stood up for each other in the army.

He had just figured out why Jimmie looked so different. It wasn't just that he was dead; it was because he didn't have that big sloppy smile on his face.

When Sam surfaced, the minister was telling everyone to turn left on County Road 16, and that it was right ahead.

Sam figures he'll just follow.

He gets in line behind a green Stratus. A man is driving, and a woman with long blonde hair is in the passenger seat.

Nice looking woman Sam cackles. *Not dead yet.*

Someone from the funeral parlour wedges a white and blue funeral sign under the hood of the car in front, and then under Sam's hood. He checks his mirror. Behind him is a white car with a man driving, no passengers. Behind the white car are maybe five other cars.

In about ten minutes, they turn onto the 401. The man in the green Stratus rides his brakes. It's a lousy habit, but it makes him easy to follow. The procession picks up speed, and pretty soon they're doing eighty. Sam sees something white fly out from between the cars. Then the funeral sign flies off the hood of the Stratus, does a flip over the roof, and disappears from sight. Another funeral sign goes flying past. His own sign stays put.

About three miles later, a car cuts in between him and the Stratus.

"Ignorant bastard," Sam says out loud. "Should know better than to cut into a funeral procession."

Three minutes later he's straining to catch the brake lights of the Stratus. Finally, he spots it over in the middle lane and slides in behind. The white car and the rest of the procession follows. The woman with the long blonde hair is driving now, but she rides the brakes as bad as her husband.

Probably her husband taught her to drive. They should've asked me. I wouldn't mind giving her a lesson or two. He chuckles to himself, thinking about what he would teach her.

Hold on, hold on. Sam shifts in his seat. *You don't change drivers when you're doing eighty on the 401.* Now a kid's face pops up in the back window. There wasn't any kid in that car before. This Sam knows for sure.

Christ! He's following the wrong car, and everyone else is following him.

What the hell is he gonna do? Everyone else is following him, and he has no idea where he's going.

Sam jumps on the accelerator. He keeps the old Monte Carlo in great shape, does most of the work himself, and he knows he can outrun these guys. Ahead of him, one of those 18-wheelers is barreling along. Sam flies up behind it, pulls over into the left lane, clears the truck, and pulls back into the middle lane. A family camper is in front of him now, and he blows his horn insistently. Eventually, the camper pulls over, and Sam zooms past, catching a glimpse of an upright finger. He pulls into the left lane and presses his foot to the floor. He passes a few more cars and another large rig, then pulls back into the middle lane and immediately into the right lane.

That should do it.

Nothing to do now but drive back to T.O. He doesn't have the faintest idea where Ogden is. He'll call it a day. He'll miss the reception, but it can't be helped. Too bad about the pies and cookies.

Sam glances into the rear view mirror. To his amazement he sees the white car with the funeral sign behind him. The driver is wiping his face. Behind the white car Sam can see a few other cars with funeral signs. *Jesus, how did they keep up with that?* And what is he going to do now? No way is he going to pull over and admit what he was doing.

An exit sign for Highway 2 comes, and Sam's brain is clicking away. He knows there's an old graveyard down this way. He remembers it from when he was visiting Jimmie. They went there for a beer. Marjorie didn't allow smoking in her house, and you sure couldn't have a beer without a smoke.

Now, if only his luck turns.

Sam pulls off the 401 onto Highway 2, and drives more sedately. Violet Road, the cut off is called. Nothing wrong with his memory. *There it is.* The cemetery is about a mile down, he remembers. It's an old dirt road. The Monte Carlo bumps over the ruts, and the dust billows up.

For a minute Sam contemplates making another get-away. He decides against it. He doesn't want to rip the bottom out of the Monte Carlo. He tries to think about what he's going to tell everyone when there's no funeral at the bone yard. After a few minutes, he decides he'll say they must have beat the rest of the procession. If he stays near the entrance maybe he can sneak out after a bit.

Five minutes later the grave yard comes into sight, and, jeeze, there's something going on there. Sam grins with delight. All the cars are parked on the left, and Sam pulls over to the right and gets out. The white car pulls up behind him. At the gate, the driver of the white car gives Sam a solemn nod and murmurs something about being grateful that Sam knew where he was going. Sam puts his head down, swipes at his eyes, and blows his nose loudly. The other followers look away tactfully; they know he and Jimmie go way back. They all move toward the little band of mourners already there.

Sam backs quietly out of the grave yard. He moves faster than he has in many years. He gets into the Monte Carlo, closes the door quietly, and pulls out onto the dirt road. About a mile along he hangs a left at the crossroad, and soon finds himself back out on Highway 2.

Ten minutes later, Sam starts to think about who is being buried back there in the Violet graveyard. He wonders when his half of the mourners will discover that they are at the wrong grave site, and what their reaction will be.

Sam thinks of Jimmie again. He pulls the car into a driver's rest stop, folds his arms over the steering wheel, and laughs till he wheezes. Jesus, Jimmie would have loved it.

He hears Jimmie's big laugh for the last time.

Growth

I WAS DESPERATE, ABSOLUTELY DESPERATE. That's why I did it.

My support group wouldn't have understood it at all. For that matter, some of them thought I shouldn't even be in the group. They made that clear on that last evening I was there. In the middle of me talking about how difficult it was that I couldn't go dancing anymore, Melissa jumped out of her chair and started screaming at me.

"Your toes, your toes," she screamed. "Look at me, I lost my freakin' arm, and you're whining about your toes."

The group leader tried to restore calm, but soon everyone was standing up, screaming about how their loss was worse than the next person's loss.

That's when I got up and walked out.

The group leader called me the next day to encourage me to return. She said that I had as much right as anyone there to grieve my loss. I declined to return. In retrospect, I wish I had. They might have given me some good advice.

It's true that losing a couple toes is nothing compared to losing a leg or an arm. But still, it affected me. I lurched slightly when I walked. I couldn't go out dancing, as I mentioned earlier. I couldn't wear my gorgeous Italian shoes. And I used to be so proud of my feet, my little feet with their high arches and pink toes, and no bunions.

I hadn't thought anything about it when the pedicurist sneezed on my feet. Then I got what I thought was a minor infection in my toenail. It wasn't until I got a diagnosis of necrotizing fasciitis, and decided to sue, that I found out the Pedicure Palace was closed and all the technicians had disappeared.

So I was desperate.

I saw the ad in one of those health magazines. You know, the ones that feature 95-year old grandmothers with thick silver hair climbing in the Andes, healthy cheesecake, and sex forevermore. It was right below the ad for beta carotene juice.

"Grow your limbs back," it enticed. "Research lab is looking for 80 people to participate in an experiment to test a new drug. Gene research on centipedes and pollywogs indicate that it **IS** possible to grow back missing limbs." In the picture was a white haired smiling man in a lab coat.

Well, I pondered, hem'd and haw'd, went back and forth, thought about asking my mother and my friends, and finally decided to just do it. So I went down to the address listed in the ad.

I really got the creeps when I walked into that room. It was full of limbless people, including two kids with their parents. There was an older guy without a nose. Is a nose even considered a limb? Eventually, a man in a white lab coat (not the man in the ad) came into the room and started to talk to us. He told us that there had been no trials on humans, and this drug was not approved by the Canadian Drug Association. It had been tried on some cats and other animals, and had been successful. He further explained to us that the animals hadn't been injured in order to test the drug. The company was against animal testing, but the drug had been used to help animals who were already injured. Next, he told us about possible side effects; dry mouth, pain and/or itching in the missing limbs, sometimes depression. None of this bothered me. I already had phantom pain in the lost toes, I was already depressed, and what was a little more pain and a dry mouth compared to what I had lost?

After that, we were told we would have to sign a release guaranteeing that we wouldn't sue the company, not that there would ever be any need to sue. At this point about 20 people, including the parents with their kids, left. I stayed.

We were told that we would have to take the medication with lots of water one hour before we ate in the morning. For the second time, the doctor explained about the possible side effects, and about signing the releases. A few more people left, and by now there were about 50 people still there.

After that, each of us had individual interviews with a nurse, during which the information was repeated for the third time. I signed the release. I asked how long before we would see results. The nurse didn't know. She advised me that if I had any doubts I should leave now. I have no idea how many people left at the end of the individual interviews.

I took the medication home and got up an hour earlier each morning to take it. I figured it was worth every minute. I wanted my toes back.

I examined my feet every night, but three months passed without any results.

One morning though, I had a hell of a shock. I was doing my breast self-examination in the shower, and I discovered a lump.

I couldn't believe it. First I lose my toes, now I'm probably going to lose my right breast. Well, you can bet I made an appointment with my doctor right away, and he confirmed it; there was a growth. He advised me not to panic. He booked a mammogram . I went for that, and the results were completely unsatisfactory, not to mention painful. It only confirmed was that there was a lump.

Then I went for another test, where they used a little rolling ball to bring up a picture of the lump on a TV screen. Then, back to the doctor. Well, there was nothing conclusive, so we discussed the options: lumpectomy, mastectomy, radiation, chemotherapy. What a list. We finally decided on a lumpectomy; that way, if it was benign, that would be it. On the other hand, if it was malignant, the surgeon would take out whatever was necessary right then and there. The lump was growing at a frightening rate. Surgery was quickly booked. I wavered between being convinced that it was just a cyst, and the dreadful thought that it was cancer, and that I would wake up without my right breast. I couldn't concentrate on anything, couldn't settle down to anything.

My doctor supplied me with a note about stress, and I got some time off work.

By this time, I wasn't even thinking of my missing toes. Taking the drug had become automatic, like taking my vitamins.

Time somehow became strange, and the day of the surgery was both too fast and too slow in arriving.

You can bet I was petrified. My mom and my sister, Lisa, came with me. Lisa and I have never been close, but I was sure glad she was there that day. She took charge, held my hand, and plumped up my pillows, and kept my mom calm— a major accomplishment.

I remember being wheeled into surgery, and the next thing I remembered was waking up in the recovery room. I had always heard that's how it goes. Beneath the bandages I could feel that I still had a breast. I was so relieved when the nurses reassured me that the lump was benign, and I had only a little 'dip' in the underside of my breast where it had been. If I had been capable of leaping out of bed and dancing around the room, I would have.

The worst was over, I thought.

There was no way I could have predicted what happened next.

No way.

The doctor visited me a few days later, took a look at the incision in my breast, and announced that it was healing well. I was feeling pretty good by that time, congratulating myself that I had come through something serious in the best possible way.

Then he said it, as he was going out the door. I'll never forget his exact words.

"You're a lucky girl," he said. "That lump was benign, so no worries. We'll just keep an eye on the breast, the other one too. Make sure you keep doing your BSE. It was pretty strange looking thing though, that thing we removed. It looked like a couple of toes, complete with toe nails. Not malignant though, that's the main thing."

Now I'm home, bed rest prescribed for a while, and Lisa is coming in after work to make me something to eat each day.

I tried to call the company that gave me that medication.

"The number you have called is not in service," a mechanical voice said.

And now I've got this freaking lump growing out of my hip.

It doesn't take a doctor to tell me what that is.

Fearless

I'M HALFWAY TO THE DOOR when I realize I've forgotten my overnight bag. I go back. There's a woman coming toward me, an elderly white lady. I glance at her, then look away immediately. I know how I look to old ladies, particularly old white ladies, and here we are in the underground parking, where women need to be cautious anyway.

Normally, I wear a suit. Then I'm still a large black man, but obviously a professional, therefore safe. Today I'm dressed casual, shorts and a muscle shirt, with a few tattoos on display. I'm a weight lifter from way back, and usually these muscles are covered up. But this evening Mariella and I are having a casual evening, a few beers on the balcony, a little television.

When I get to the elevators, the woman, who is carrying a purse and a large manila envelope, is waiting to get on. I try to look as unaggressive as possible. I keep my arms close to my body and my stance narrow. When the elevator comes, I step back politely to let her go on first, and stand against the opposite wall trying to look as small as possible, which isn't easy considering I'm 210 lbs. I must look enormous to my elevator companion who must be all of 100 lbs and frail.

I keep my eyes to the floor, but the elevator has barely started when I notice a small brown lump in the corner diagonal to me. It's disgusting. Someone has let their dog toilet in the elevator and didn't pick it up. And these are relatively new, high-end condos.

But then the lump moves, and, oh, shit, it's a mouse. Immediately, I'm five years old again, tangled in the bed sheets with a mouse, and my two brothers laughing at my terror.

I'm staring at the mouse, paralyzed, when it makes a sudden dash at me.

I shriek and try to get out of the way, but there is only one direction to run in this little space. With a loud thump, I hit the wall next to the old woman. She shrieks.

The end to this episode flashes through my mind, and I see it as if watching a movie. I've given the old woman a heart attack, the mouse has given me a heart attack, and in the final scene, the elevator door slides open, two bodies on the floor, and the mouse emerges victorious, smoking a miniature cigar. Mouse 2, People 0.

I glance at the lady beside me, so neat in a flowery dress, with her hair in a bun. She looks back at me.

"It's a mouse, dear," she says.

I want to tell her I know what it is, but what comes out of my mouth instead is, "I...I...I..."

"Well, we're almost at my floor," she says. "Why don't you just get off with me and then catch the next elevator up?"

I look at the mouse, positioned right at the door.

"Oh," says the woman.

Then she takes her large brown envelope and begins to chase the mouse into the opposite corner, actually saying "shoo, shoo", to it. When it's in the corner, she barricades the mouse with the envelope, and tells me to stand by the door so I can get off as soon as the elevator stops.

"But hold the door for me dear, because this is my floor" she tells me.

And that is what happens. I get off and hold the door for her, and she walks off, perfectly composed. I let the doors close. The mouse is the only passenger now.

The woman takes a look at me, then asks me if I want to sit down. There is nothing to sit on, so I just back up against the wall. I can feel the sweat running down out of my hairline.

"Don't faint, dear," says the woman. "I'm not sure I could hold you up."

Is that a smirk I hear in her voice?

She puts her hand out to me and introduces herself as Evelyn. I tell her my name is Nigel.

Evelyn's hand is warm and boney. She rummages in her purse and pulls out a little package of Kleenex. She hands one to me, remarking on how humid it is. I use it to wipe the sweat off my face.

"Now, dear, are you going to be all right getting back on the elevator, or do you want me to come with you for protection?" says Evelyn. She is laughing at me!

I look at her blue eyes magnified behind her glasses and laugh till I'm almost falling over. Evelyn is laughing too, and her laugh is surprisingly hearty.

"Evelyn, I'm taking the stairs,"

"Okay dear."

The next morning, Mariella and I are coming down in the elevator when it stops at the 12th floor, and, of course, Evelyn gets on.

"Good morning! Isn't it a beautiful day?" she says.

"Indeed, it is," replies Mariella. "It's so beautiful that Nigel and I are just going out to try flat-boarding. But I have to admit I'm a little nervous."

"Oh goodness," says Evelyn. "Don't worry about it. Your boyfriend will take care of you. With muscles like that, I'm sure he isn't afraid of anything."

"You're right," says Mariella, patting my arm. "The man is absolutely fearless."

Evelyn grins.

I grin too.

Dianne's Gift

SO, HERE I AM, AND what do I do next? Put one foot in front of the other, I say to myself, and then I take a big breath and go in the front door and up the stairs to the left, following the signs.

"Welcome to Dress for Success," the woman at the desk says. "You must be Elizabeth."

I nod.

"We have some forms to fill out," she says, and gestures for me to have a seat. Name, address (I give the shelter address), and the usual information, but when we come to what size clothes, I have no idea. I haven't shopped for clothes in years. Also, the question about what I need; where was the box that said "No clue"?

"Don't worry about it," the lady says. "Dianne will be your fashion consultant, and she's very good at what she does."

My fashion consultant?

Dianne is a black woman, and I feel a little touch of nerves. I've never talked to a black woman before. There just aren't any black people where I come from, up in farming country. I'm sure there are black people who are farmers, just none where I come from. Gordon always said that all black men were rapists and all black women were whores. One day, I said to him that if all black women were whores then black men didn't need to be rapists. I didn't really believe that, but every once in a while I got tired of his belittling everybody. Chinese people, Indians, Blacks, women, men who worked in offices—Gordon hated everybody.

"What the fuck do you know?" Gordon said. "You haven't been off this goddam farm in years."

And he was right. He had the keys to the truck and there was no way I could get my hands on them. So, I hadn't been off the farm in years.

"Hi," says Dianne, and I say "hi" back and decide I will talk to her like I talk to anyone else. After all, the numbers of pigment cells in your skin don't have anything to do with the way you talk.

Then I tell Dianne that I don't have much money. I know the worker at the shelter said the clothes are free, but I can't believe that. But Dianne says not to worry about the money, the clothes are indeed free. I'm so relieved. I have no idea how much anything costs anymore. Gordon picked up anything I needed in town. He said that it made more sense for him to pick up whatever we needed than for him to come back to the farm and get me and go back out again. Once I told him that I would like to go into town for a bit, but of course he told me that a wife belongs in the home, and the apples were ripe, so why didn't I get busy for a change and make some apple pies or something. And what was I bitching about, he worked all day and took care of the milk cows, while I sat around watching television, so what did I have to complain about.

Dianne asks me what name I want to use, and I make a decision right then. I will never be Lizzy again. Lizzy is a scared woman, a woman who makes apple pies because her husband likes them, because if she does what her husband likes maybe he'll be nicer to her. I tell Dianne I am called Elizabeth.

We go through a curtain and I see rows and rows of clothes on racks. I'm gawking at the clothes because there's so much. Dresses, jackets, blouses, pants.

"Now, you're going for a job interview. What's the job?" Dianne asks.

I tell her it's a reception job. I don't say so, but I know there's nothing else I know how to do right now. Melanie at the shelter got me the job interview. It's a travel agency, and basically they want someone who can smile, bring coffee to the clients, give them some brochures, and generally make them feel comfortable while they're waiting for the travel agent. This is something I can do. I have lots of practice pleasing people. Well, pleasing Gordon anyway, and he wasn't that easy to please.

Dianne asks me if I would feel more comfortable in a skirt or dress, or in dress pants. I think a bit and tell her pants. I haven't worn a skirt or dress in years. Dianne starts going through the racks. She pulls out a pair of black dress pants, a plain white blouse, a blue and white patterned blouse, and a black jacket. I'm in the change room sliding out of my sweat pants when she hands me a skirt over the top. It's a straight, red skirt, and before I can say anything, Dianne asks me to at least try it on, even if I don't like it right now.

The first clothes I try on are the black pants and the patterned blouse, which has short sleeves. When I step out of the change room and raise my arm to tuck in the tag, I know Dianne has noticed the scars on the back of my arm, the ring pattern, but she says nothing.

I look in the mirror, and I'm shocked: I didn't know that I could look like this, like a business woman. But I don't know if I can wear short sleeves, and let people see this scar. Will people keep asking me how I got the scar? I can't tell them I call the scar "Gordon's gift".

Dianne suggests I go back into the change room and try on the other clothes, including the red skirt, looking at the different combinations, with and without the jacket. I marvel at how many combinations I can make.

Most people would not consider this scar a gift. Most people would recognize the burn scars made by the rings of a stove burner. But, three years ago, this scar started me thinking of escape. This scar told me to make a plan.

I was careful, very, very careful. I started selling eggs, putting a home-made sign at the bottom of the lane when Gordon was away, and making sure I got it back hidden before he got home. I knew I was taking a risk with the eggs, but I emphasized to each customer that if the sign wasn't out,

I didn't have any eggs to sell, and they shouldn't come up the lane.

But, the eggs are how I got most of my funds. Of course, I also hoarded any spare change Gordon left in his pockets when I did the laundry and picked up a few bucks out of his coat pockets when he went to bed. When he came home drunk, I could take a bit more; he would never remember what he had in his wallet. I hid my cash in the kitchen cupboard. It was safe there. Gordon never opened a kitchen cupboard in the ten years I lived with him. Little by little, my stash grew.

One Saturday, this older lady, Emma, drove up the lane to buy eggs, as she did every few weeks. Emma was friendly and liked to chat with me when she bought eggs. She told me that she worked at the bank in town, had worked there for about 30 years, and was ready to retire. She was a large woman, but she looked good with her short white hair fluffed out around her face.

Emma asked me about the scars on my arm, and I told her about how clumsy I was, and that I was always hurting myself. She just kind of nodded her head and went "uh, huh". I don't think she believed me, but all she said was to be more careful.

One day I didn't have the sign out because it was Saturday, and Gordon was home, so I don't know why she came. But when Gordon came out of the house, glaring, and telling her she was trespassing, she seemed to figure it out right away. She immediately apologized, pretended that she had gotten lost and come up the wrong lane. She asked for forgiveness for an old, confused lady, and when she reached out to shake my hand, I could feel a business card transfer from her palm to mine.

When Gordon went out the next day, I called the number on the card. It was Emma's business number at the bank. She said only that she would help me when I asked for it. She continued to come and buy eggs every few weeks, when the sign was outside, and always asked if I still had her phone number.

So Emma is the person I called a year later, and she was as good as her word. She picked me up and bought me a train ticket to Toronto, telling me to save my funds for when I got to the city. She gave me an address to a woman's shelter, a few bucks for food and transportation, and now I'm here.

That's why I call this scar "Gordon's gift" because these scars are what started me thinking about how to get away.

When I come out and look at myself dressed in the red skirt, the white blouse and the black jacket, I can't help it, I smile at myself. I know Gordon would walk right by me on the street; he would never recognize me.

"Now, you smile like that in the interview, and you'll get the job for sure. You have a wonderful smile," Dianne says.

I feel tears flood my eyes at her kindness.

"Let's look at shoes," Dianne says, and we both look down.

Although I'm skinny, my feet are big. Once Gordon came home and told me he had a new pair of shoes for me. It turned out that he had bought himself new shoes, but then he used a magic marker to draw laces and a bow on the shoe box and presented it to me.

"I'll get you the other foot next time I'm in town," he roared, delighted with his wit. No doubt that made a good story in the bar that evening.

"Size ten, same as me." Dianne guesses, and she's right. We both look at her shoes. She has on plain black shoes, with a little heel. Dianne tells me that larger sizes can be a little difficult, but she's hopeful they have something. I really hope so too, because I only have the old ones I'm wearing, the sole detaching from the uppers.

Dianne tells me I can change back into my own clothes, and she'll go and take a look for the shoes. Before I can go back into the change room, the lady from the front desk comes by. She tells me to hold on a bit, and in a few minutes she comes back with a scarf in pale blue and white. She puts the scarf around my neck, and the outfit looks even better. Than we hold the scarf up against the patterned blouse, then the white blouse, and we have some discussion about whether I could wear the scarf with the patterned blouse. The lady shows me how to tie the scarf so only the blue part shows, and then so that only the white part shows. I'm learning so much that most women my age already know. I go back into the change room and get into my old clothes, which now feel horribly shabby.

My new clothes won't look so good if Dianne can't find me some shoes. And I'm kind of worried because the scarf thing took a while, so I know she must be having difficulty finding shoes. If there are no shoes I will have to use some of the money I saved to get a pair. I can ask the ladies here where to go to get some at a good price.

I'm changed and waiting outside the room for what seems like forever when she returns. Dianne holds a pair of low heeled black shoes. She tells me to try them on. I do, and they fit. I can't believe my luck, because they feel new. I take them off and look at the bottoms, and they have hardly a scuff mark on them. I'm elated. Everything is going my way. I can feel my confidence soar. I'll smile at the job interview tomorrow, and I'll get the job. I know I will. This evening I'll get someone at the shelter to ask me interview type questions, so I can be ready.

We go to the front, and Dianne packs the clothes in tissue and into a nice bag, except for the shoes. I throw my old shoes in the garbage and wear my new ones. It looks like I've been shopping for real. I can't stop saying "thank you" to both these women. Thank you for their time, thank you for the clothes, thank you for their kindness.

Dianne tells me I'm the last client of the day and she'll come down the stairs with me and lock the front door. I'm still saying "thank you" when Dianne opens the door for me and tells me to watch the step at the door sill. "Good night, good luck tomorrow," Dianne calls cheerfully as she locks the door behind me.

I look back at Dianne. And I feel myself gasp. Instead of her low heeled black shoes Dianne now has on a pair of running shoes. They're nice looking shoes, but they are definitely not the low black heels she had on earlier. I peer down at my own feet.

And all I can think is: Dianne's gift.

If Ever You Need a Poltergeist

I'M HALF ASLEEP WHEN I hear the footsteps come up the stairs. I raise my head and strain my eyes toward the door. I really don't expect to see anyone there. I absolutely don't expect to see what I do see.

I've heard those footsteps coming up the stairs a hundred times, and there is never anyone there.

But this time it's different.

A long, long time ago, something must have happened in this house around the months leading up to Christmas. Something bad? I don't know. But something.

I've lived in this house for almost fourteen years, and I'm no longer afraid when I hear footsteps coming up the stairs. Like anything that you experience repeatedly, it had lost it threat, or promise. Like getting use to holding a snake, or seeing a mouse. Aversion therapy, I think it's called. No, wait. That's not it. Anyway, therapy for a phobia, whatever that's called.

Now I'm no longer worried about the sound of someone coming up the stairs, or shaking the bed, or stirring the wind chimes that are hanging in the corner.

I should have been.

Believe me, when I first moved in to this old house, I was afraid. It was just weird: the bed shaking, the feeling that someone was in the room, and the non-existent intruders coming up the stairs at night.

After I had spent about three sleepless weeks in my new home, I thought about selling. But I had just used my life savings as a down payment, and I couldn't bear the thought of going through the selling, the moving, and the bottom had just dropped out of the real estate market. And I liked the house. It was old and small, and had only two closets, but the bedrooms had dormers, there were odd cubby spaces, and a good size backyard. And it was all mine.

I could take my time and fix it up as my pay increased. First on the list was planting a garden.

I decided I would just stay for now and see what happened.

A year passed, and nothing much happened. At least, nothing more than what had already happened. There was no poltergeist activity, no flinging around of small or large objects, no daytime activity, and no appearances of ghostly images. Sometimes, when I was having a late tea with a friend, they would hear steps going up the stairs, but that was easy enough to work with. I could see them question themselves and decide it was their imagination – after all, the sound was faint.

When Al, and later Will, stayed overnight they didn't notice anything. It's always easy to attribute a small noise or movement to the person you're with. Really, after so many years, I had just gotten used to the disturbances, if they could be called disturbances when, in fact, they no longer disturbed me.

When I thought seriously about it, I realized that nothing malignant had ever happened. There was activity, but always low keyed, and never threatening.

However, I unconsciously started to notice trends. Whatever 'it' was, was fairly quiet during the summer months, but became more active around September, and most active in the months leading up to Christmas. After Christmas, the activity lessened and was only occasional over the rest of the year, until September rolled around again.

I only half believed there was some presence in my home until the summer a van stopped outside and a woman, who introduced herself as Nancy, asked if she could show her adult daughter the house they had lived in when her daughter was a small child. I invited them in, and Nancy and I had some general conversation about the neighbourhood, and the inconvenience of living in a house with only two closets.

Nancy turned out to be a really practical woman, having raised two kids with little storage space, and offered some decent storage solutions. Then, to my surprise, she asked me if I had experienced any strange happenings in the front bedroom. I asked Nancy what she meant.

"Well, the bed used to shake at night," she said. "I would get out of the bed and put my hand on it, and it would still be shaking. "But, Gary, my husband, didn't believe in that sort of thing, and nothing seemed to happen when he was home."

It was validating, knowing that someone else had experienced these ghostly visitations.

Now, after fourteen years, I simply accepted the disruptions. And I loved my little house. I had put in some flowers, done some painting, replaced the knob and tube wiring, and had a little collection of my nicely framed travel pictures on the front room wall.

But then an idea gradually occurred to me. I wondered if the spirit, or ghost, or phantom, or whatever it was, might be suffering. I questioned whether this being, this entity, was caught between worlds, between the world I lived in and whatever world waited on the other side.

I checked online and called the Centre for the Study of the Paranormal. It was an interesting call, and the woman, Jean, was very helpful.

"Well, talk to it," Jean said.

"Out loud?"

"Yup. Speak out loud. Tell him, or her, that they have loved ones waiting on the other side, that they've been waiting a long time, and it's time to cross over and join their loved ones."

"Okay," I said doubtfully. "But I don't mind if they stay. We've gotten along together for fourteen years now."

"So, tell them they can stay if they want to."

"Okay."

Frankly, I couldn't imagine myself talking out loud to an empty room, but if the spirit needed help, I would try.

A couple weeks later, near the end of December, I did just that. When I felt some presence in the room, I sat up in bed. I spoke to the empty room. I told the room that the year was 2008, that I didn't know how long they had been in this house, but that people were waiting on the other side, people who loved them and wanted to be with them. I also said that if they wanted to stay, they were welcome to do so. They and I had lived here in harmony for fourteen years now, and could continue to live in harmony. They were welcome to stay.

I can't say I felt anything different. I can't say that I thought anything, human or phantom, was listening.

I can say I felt stupid talking to an empty room, especially since I repeated it all several times. I had no idea why I did that. Did I think the spirit was deaf, or stupid, or couldn't understand English?

For a few weeks after that I tried to be more aware of the level of activity, wondering if my strange conversation had reached anybody. I tried to figure out if there was less activity or more. I thought it might be somewhat less, but I really couldn't decide.

But then, something happened.

Later, the police complimented me, saying I had put up a terrific fight. I couldn't remember.

This time the footsteps on the stairs were real. When I lifted my head from the pillow, there was someone standing there. A man.

For a few seconds my brain didn't register. Had I called up the spirit by talking to it, made it into a real person somehow? My brain couldn't take in what my eyes were seeing.

Then he was by the bed, and I knew he was real. He was talking to me, or to himself, in a low nasty voice, telling me I was a slut, I was going to get what I deserved, that I wanted it, to admit that I wanted it. In terror I pulled the blankets up over myself. It was the wrong thing to do. Instead of being upright I was already down. When I screamed he punched me in the face. I felt a tooth come loose and start to slide down my throat. Idiotically, I wondered if it was a real tooth or one of my expensive implants. That was my last thought.

When I woke up, I was on a cot in a hospital hallway with the taste of blood in my mouth. I was disoriented, and the pain in my face was incredible. Later, I discovered my nose had been broken.

A policewoman was by the bed, along with my sister, Donna, who was listed on my cell as my emergency contact. Donna stayed with me while the nurse did a physical exam, and started the rape kit. It turned out I hadn't been raped. All my injuries were on my face; there was no other bruising anywhere. I didn't understand that. Why didn't he rape me when he had all the power?

Eventually, I pieced together more information from the policewoman.

My neighbour, when he went out to bring his trash can to the curb, had heard a huge commotion coming from my place. He immediately dialed 911, but even as he was dialing, a man burst out of my front door, running as if the devil were after him. He was staggering; he seemed to be injured.

I was told that the police picked him up several blocks away. He was suffering from cuts to his hands and had a large gash across his face. His jeans were ripped along the thigh where he was bleeding.

My neighbour, bless him, stayed with me until the police and ambulance arrived.

In the hospital the policewoman congratulated me on putting up a successful defense.

"You have to make a choice when you're in this kind of terrible situation," she said. "Sometimes fighting makes things worse, sometimes it saves you. But one thing we know is that women who defend themselves are better off emotionally than those who choose not to. And obviously, you made the right choice. We got the guy, and frankly, he looks worse than you do."

She grinned, and fist-bumped me.

But, I knew I hadn't defended myself: I knew that I had passed out when I'd been punched in the face. I told this to the policewoman, and she said that the mind has a way of blocking out trauma. She suggested that I get some counselling, and better locks on my doors.

A few days later I returned home with my sister, who had called a locksmith to come and put extra locks on my house.

I couldn't believe my eyes when I opened the door. It looked like some kind of horror scene from a movie.

Donna and I picked our way through a trail of wreckage and blood, beginning in my room and going down the stairs and out the front door. The heavy chair in my bedroom was lying on its side. My travel pictures had been torn from the walls and lay with the glass shattered on the rugs, my book case was overturned, the foot stool was tumbled by the front door. The damage was overwhelming.

I wondered if my travel pictures could be saved and reframed. I wondered if the blood on the carpet could be cleaned. I wondered if I could live there anymore.

"Oh my god," Donna said, putting her arm around my shoulders. "I don't believe it. It's like you went mad." She looked at me with some awe. "Shit. I'm never going to annoy you again. Listen, you can stay with me as long as you want, and I'll go halves with you on getting a professional to clean it up. I owe you, Sis, you've done a lot for me in the past. So just let me do this."

It took a lot of thinking, but eventually I figured it out. And then I knew it. I knew I had been right when I had spoken that night and said that the spirit was welcome to stay.

There had been only two people in my home the night of the attack: myself and my attacker.

And one unknown who had stuck around.

Flash Fiction

I CAN HEAR SOME GIRLS yakking away, coming along the path, and I get myself ready. Not that I'm ever not ready. But I've learned to be careful, and I wait, and it's a good thing that I do, because there's a man with these girls. A big man too, and if one of these girls belong to him it won't go over well. So I smile and nod, and keep my hands in my jacket pocket and my pants zipped. I've cultivated a little beard lately. I see one of the two girls glance at me and away, and smile to herself.

Too bad she wasn't alone. The encounter would be a lot sweeter if she were. If she didn't have a man to protect her she wouldn't be walking around thinking she was Miss Queen Bee.

But that's okay. There's a lot more girls in this park.

The next girl I encounter on the pathway is not really a girl but an old woman. She must be in her early forties, at least, and I think about displaying, but decide it's not worth it. Women that old don't get scared; they get indignant, or outraged, and usually have their wits about them to call the police.

So I just smile at her, and she smiles back, seeing a thirty something, well-dressed man taking a stroll after his busy work day. She's probably thinking that I'm some poor, overworked husband, maybe with a toddler at home, and trying to take a break after a strenuous day. And she wouldn't be far from the truth. I'm a financial advisor, making good money for my clients and better money for myself. It allows me a good life style, with a nice condo close to the park. No wife or babies though, and my mother keeps telling me how she had two kids in school by the time she was my age. I want to go "yeah, yeah, I know" when she goes on about it, but I just keep my mouth shut.

I hear some girls coming along the path again, and as always, I wait till I know who is there. There was one time when I saw only girls, and then found out there was a man coming along behind them, and when the girls got hysterical the man came running up, playing the big hero. I had to make tracks fast that time, but in a way, it added to the thrill of it all. I got away, but after that I noticed there were some uniforms walking around the trails for a while. Well, they weren't really in uniform, but you could tell by the size of them, really big men, and I didn't like that. They could do me some serious damage.

A few days later, I saw some home-made notices in the park that there was a flasher, and I laughed to myself. Pretty nice that I'm scaring girls when I'm not even in the park.

Well, girls, I'm available today.

That poster business didn't last too long though. The police didn't have the resources to look for a flasher when they have people with guns, and drive-by shootings to attend to. They probably thought it was pretty funny too. After all, the cops are men. Sure there's some women now on traffic or on a desk, but it's the men who do the real work.

And the posters soon got rained on and disappeared.

This time it's good. Two girls, probably not yet twenty, walking, giggling, not paying attention. Two silly girls. I'm hard. I pull it out, and this time I do something different. I make a little jerky movement towards the girls, as if I'm going to run at them. It works well. The girls gasp, shriek, and take off, not even waiting to see if the other one is okay. If I were to grab one of them, the other one wouldn't even know it until it was too late. Maybe next time.

That felt pretty good.

Girls today think they're so smart becoming doctors and lawyers and even financial advisors. These two don't feel so smart now.

A couple of men are walking fast along the trail now and ask me if I heard some girls screaming. I tell them I heard a commotion, but I don't know what it was, and I did see some old bum in the bushes a little further up. The two men thank me and walk on rapidly, looking now for some old bum.

I'm the last person anyone would think to look for; a thirtyish man, dressed in business casual. People remember what they presume to be true. Flashers are dirty old men, not young, attractive men.

I feel pretty good now and I'm heading toward home. I might or might not see more girls on this path, but one thing is sure: I scored one for the men today.

There are now two more girls who know they really don't have control. They know now that no matter what career they choose, no matter how important they become in the world, a man can always teach them that they have something to fear. It's men who have power, and girls will only have what the men allow them to have. And I can teach them that.

And maybe, someday, with an even better lesson than I did today.

Introduction to Hunger:

MY MOTHER, YVONNE, WAS BORN in 1916 and placed in an orphanage (Hospice de Levis), at the age of five, along with some of her brothers and sisters, when her mother died. When she was ten, Yvonne left this institution to live with a family who abused her physically and emotionally for the next seven years. She carried scars of the physical abuse all her life. She was able to leave that family when she was 17, and worked for another family, who treated her very kindly, until she was 21.

Yvonne was homeless during the depression in Quebec and survived by doing whatever domestic work she could find, sleeping in churches when she couldn't afford a bed.

The following three stories are fiction based on her life. Mom died in July 2013 at the age of 96.

Hunger One

THE HOUSE SMELLS WONDERFUL, EVEN MY little room in the attic. I've been baking Christmas cookies for days, and even decorated some of them with red and green icing, and these are the ones that hang from the tree.

Louise and Muriel made garlands with popcorn and pretty wooden beads for the tree, and Mrs. Lapointe even bought some of those glass ornaments. They cost ten cents each. Everyone was so careful putting them on the tree. And there's a glass star on the top. It looks really beautiful.

Mrs. Lapointe and Muriel went into St Michele De Bellechase and got their hair marcelled. Muriel looks more like her mom every day. They are both large women with broad faces and small eyes, and with their hair done the same it's easy to see that they are mother and daughter. Louise doesn't look like either her mother or her grandmother. I guess she looks like her father. I've never seen him.

The guests are in the front room listening to Fibber McGee and Molly and laughing because Mr. McGee wants to have a white Christmas tree. He ruins the floor trying to paint the green tree with white paint. Mrs. Lapointe, Muriel and Louise are in there too.

Mr. Lapointe is sitting by the wood stove, reading a paper, quiet as always. He's a large man too, but not solid like his wife, just kind of soft all around.

Yesterday, Louise was telling me about some of our Christmas traditions. She said that having a tree for Christmas was a German tradition and only became popular when Queen Victoria put one up as a gift to her husband, Prince Albert, who was German. That was such a kind thing for the Queen to do.

Louise is nine now, and sometimes she tries to teach me to read, but we have to be careful because Mrs. Lapointe would be really mad if she found out. So would Muriel.

On the radio Mr. McGee insults someone named Alice, and the guests laugh along with the radio audience. I smile.

I take the bread pudding out of the oven and set it on a cutting board and pick a little piece off the edge. I'm just going to put it in my mouth when something hits me across the back of my head with such force that my forehead smashes into the cupboards in front of me.

"Oh, geeze, Vera," says Mr. Lapointe. "Don't hit her like that."

"I'll hit her however I want," says Mrs. Lapointe. She does. She's been hitting me since I came here, and Mr. Lapointe keeps on telling her not to, but she still does.

I can feel blood dripping into my eyes. Mr. Lapointe gets a clean rag, wets it and gives it to me.

When Mother Superior told me I'd be leaving the orphanage, I hoped I would be with someone kind. But that didn't happen.

I remember sitting in the hallway when Mr. and Mrs. Lapointe came to get me, and I heard Mother Superior talking to them in her office. She told them I should go to school, because I was only ten years old, and needed to learn to read and write.

Mrs. Lapointe said that of course they would send me to school. Mr. Lapointe didn't say anything at all.

Then they came out, and I went with them. It was a long ride to St Michele De Bellechase, and we stopped twice to rest the horse, but that was okay since it was summer and I got to look around. I had been in the orphanage since I was five years old, and I didn't remember much before that, except when Mama died, and that was very sad. So everything I saw was interesting.

When we came into town it was wonderful. There were cars in the streets and stores full of everything. We passed a building that said Holy Mother Mary School, and I got really excited because I figured that maybe this was the school I would go to. I got a little nervous because going to school in the orphanage just meant going down the stairs and lining up, and that was easy. I wondered how I would get to school here, and if I should wear the serge dress I had from the orphanage.

I was kind of worried too, because I was behind in school. I hadn't attended very much because I was sick a lot, and right then, sitting in that buggy, I made up my mind to pay lots of attention and learn to read and write and do arithmetic really well, so Mr. and Mrs. Lapointe would feel proud of me.

But the horse and buggy continued through town and we seemed to be going a long way out into the country.

"How will I get to school?" I asked. I was a little afraid to ask because in the orphanage we kept quiet unless the nuns asked us something.

"Don't be so stupid," Mrs. Lapointe said. "Do you think we got you so we could mollycoddle you? You're going to work, not to school. And don't even think about complaining. Mother Superior gave you to us. I own you, and you'll do what I say."

I had heard them tell Mother Superior that I would go to school. Wasn't it a mortal sin to lie to Mother? Would they go to hell for that?

Even though I know I shouldn't think that way, sometimes I do wish Mrs. Lapointe, and Muriel too, would go to hell. It would serve them right.

Now, I've been here seven years, and I've never gone to school. I think about it every day. I know I've forgotten some of what they taught me in the orphanage school. When I go up to my room at night I take some of the newspapers that Mr. Lapointe reads, if I can get it, and I try to read. It's really hard though. I don't know if I'm making mistakes and there's no one to tell me if I do. I've given up on learning to add and subtract, but I want to read so badly it's like something is gnawing at me inside.

And I've never seen my sisters or brothers since I've been here. I don't think they would even know where to find me.

I take the rag from Mr. Lapointe, who looks at me with sad eyes, and I hold it over the cut on my forehead.

Louise frowns at her grandmother, who ignores her.

When my cut stops bleeding, I start on the dishes. Cooking isn't too bad because we have the electricity, but I have ironing to do tonight as well, and that's the worst job of all. I have to be so careful not to overheat the flat iron on the stove; if I burn anything, I'll get hit for sure.

But tomorrow is Christmas Day, and all I'll have to do is cook and serve.

Right now, we have four guests for Christmas: Mr. and Mrs. Tremblay and their two sons, who are about eight and ten years old. Mrs. Tremblay seems to be sick; she's coughing a lot, holding an embroidered handkerchief to her mouth, and I heard Muriel whisper to her mother about consumption.

An idea starts to come to me.

I cough.

On Christmas Day I'm making the tourtière when Louise comes in from the front room where everyone else is opening gifts and hands me a package. When I open it I find a knitted hat, a little crooked, but done in many different colours, and I know that Louise has used the leftover yarn from her mama's and grand-mere's projects. Tears come into my eyes, and I push the hat into my dress pocket so no one will see it. It's the only gift I have had since I got here.

In the orphanage we all got an apple, an orange and some candies for Christmas. But here I get nothing.

Mrs. Tremblay is coughing all the time now, and I get a little scared that maybe she does have tuberculosis, and I guess Mr. Tremblay is scared too because the next day Dr. Belanger shows up. He's the new doctor, and Mrs. Lapointe doesn't like him very much because when he came last time he said that I should have more to eat, and more time off for resting. And he asked her why I had a bruise on my arm.

Dr. Belanger examines Mrs. Tremblay in her room, and when he comes down he tells Mrs. Lapointe that she just has influenza, and should get lots of rest. Then he asks me what happened to my forehead.

I don't answer. Then I pretend like I'm trying to answer and cough instead.

The doctor looks at me, then pulls out his stethoscope and comes over and puts it against my back, although Mrs. Lapointe is telling him not to do that. And I feel scared because I know he can tell with that thing that I'm not sick at all, and after he leaves Mrs. Lapointe will hit me for lying.

After the doctor listens to my breathing, he comes and puts his face close to mine, saying out loud that he needs to look at my eyes. He tells me to look at him. I do and I see him mouth "say yes".

"Yvonne," he says out loud. "Are you tired a lot?"

"Yes," I say.

"Do you cough a lot?"

"Yes."

"Are you coughing up phlegm?"

"Yes."

"Are you sweating at night?"

"Yes."

Dr. Belanger puts his stethoscope away, looking very serious, and he puts his hand on my forehead and frowns.

Then he goes over and talks to Mrs. Lapointe in a low voice.

"But I need her here. It's Christmas and there's a lot to do," I hear Mrs. Lapointe say. And then I hear the doctor talking in a low voice about contagion, and Louise, and danger, and treatment.

"I'm not paying for her to get treatment. I'm not her mother," Mrs. Lapointe says.

"No, no," the doctor says in a normal voice. "There are free clinics. Don't worry about it. I'll take her to Quebec City and get her admitted. You won't have to pay anything. But she'll need treatment for at least a year."

He turns to me and tells me to pack my stuff, and he'll come back for me in the morning. It's like he doesn't give Mrs. Lapointe time to say no.

Louise starts to cry and asks Dr. Belanger if I'm going to die, and the doctor bends down to her and tells her that he'll take good care of me and I'll soon be as good as new.

The next morning Dr. Belanger comes for me. Mrs. Lapointe and Muriel are in with the guests, but Mr. Lapointe comes out and kisses me on the forehead. I thank him for helping me. Louise comes out and hugs me, and she's crying, and I know she's the one person I will miss. I take out her hat and put it on, and she smiles a bit.

Driving in the car is very loud and very exciting. I've never been in a car before, so I'm a little scared. The wind is blowing in my face, and I can't believe how fast we're going.

We're out of sight of the house when Dr. Belanger turns to me.

"I hope you know you don't really have tuberculosis. You're healthy as a horse, just too skinny. Didn't they feed you anything?"

"I get to eat, but only after everyone else eats" I say. "Except sometimes Mr. Lapointe snuck me some extra food".

"Well, congratulations on coughing so convincingly." He grins. "I'm taking you to my mother's place in Trois Rivieres. She's getting on, and you can cook and clean for her, and help her get around. She can't pay you much, but you can eat whatever and whenever you want.'

Pay me?

"You don't have to go back to that place, ever," he says, jerking his thumb behind him.

Then he says that his mother likes it if someone reads to her, because her eyesight is starting to go, and my heart stops. I think if I can't read maybe his mother won't want me there.

"I don't know how to read," I say.

"Don't worry", he says. "She used to be a schoolmarm. She'll teach you soon enough."

I can't believe it, but as I look at him, he nods his head. "You'll learn to read." he says.

Hunger Two

"YVONNE, YVONNE," I HEAR, AND I turn over, hugging the back of the pew to make sure I don't roll off.

I would like to sleep some more, but my hunger and the cold wake me up.

It's Veronique, who was sleeping toe to toe with me on the same pew, calling to me in a kind of whisper. Cecile and Denise are in the pew behind us.

I flip my coat off me, sit up, and put the coat on. I look down at my dress, which is wrinkled, and I know it needs washing, but I haven't had the opportunity to do anything about that. When I took care of Mrs. Belanger I always kept my clothes clean. But now it's really hard in the winter, because you can't put on a wet dress and go out into this cold. So I stand up and smooth the dress down as much as I can.

I pull my old knit hat over my hair. It's multi-coloured, a little crooked, and full of memories.

Veronique gets up and smooths her dress as well, muttering to herself. Yesterday, she spilt coffee on her dress, and, like all of us, it's the only dress she has.

Veronique is from a farm outside of Levis. She's the oldest of seven kids, and when she saw that the food they'd preserved in the summer was running out she started to worry that the younger kids would be going hungry. So one morning, she put a couple baked potatoes in her dress pocket and walked away. She ended up here in Trois-Rivieres, and when Cecile and Denise saw she was alone, they befriended her.

Cecile and Denise are 25 and 23, but Veronique looks to be only about 18.

Today is Veronique's first choice of any jobs going. Tomorrow will be mine. We do this alphabetically to make sure it's fair.

The four or us make the sign of the cross, genuflect to the altar, and tiptoe to the front door. We try to be quiet because we can see there are others still sleeping.

At the front door we all complain about the cold. But it's February in Quebec, so we all know that is that.

Shivering, we slip and slide across the frozen snow to the restaurant, use the washroom and wash our faces. I use some wet paper towels and wipe off under my arms as much as I can. Then I fold a paper towel and shove it into my shoe over the hole there.

"Whew", says Cecile. "*Je suis malodorante*".

None of us have had a bath in a couple weeks, and I'm pretty sure we all smell, and are just used to it.

Cecile and Denise re-braid each other's hair. Both Veronique and I have bobbed our hair, not for the style, but for the convenience. Veronique swears she'll grow hers out again once we get a place to live. Her hair is so dark brown and even short you can see how thick and shiny it is.

We pool our resources: we make sure we have three cents for the newspaper, and that leaves enough for coffees all around and two doughnuts, which we share. We get the doughnuts with the sugar on top because we know we need the energy from the sugar.

Two doughnuts among four women isn't much. All of us are careful, making sure we don't get more than our share. It feels as if that little piece of dough is dropping through empty air to hit the bottom of my stomach. But I know the other girls are just as hungry as I am.

At the newspaper stand the headlines are much the same as yesterday: The Great Depression, the newspapers are calling it, and the prediction is that 1937 is not going to be any better than 1936 was. The estimate is that about 20% of the population is unemployed. I wonder if that takes girls and women into account or only men.

Tuberculosis is there on page two, and the newspaper tells people to use a handkerchief to cover their mouth when they sneeze and don't shake hands if they can avoid it.

The newspapers are full of thrift suggestions: how to turn the sheets, how to make a shepherd's pie in order to stretch the hamburger, which now costs 12 cents a pound. I feel my mouth water at the mention of hamburger which I haven't tasted in close to a year. If we all got jobs we could probably save 12 cents between the four of us, but we wouldn't have anywhere to cook the hamburger anyway.

The ongoing scandal of King Edward and Wallis Simpson is still a good part of the news.

Just before we turn to the job ads, I see a notice that Amelia Earhart might be planning a trip around the world. I wonder what kind of education or training you need to fly a plane. I've never even been in a plane, and probably never will be, never mind flying one.

Denise flips the paper open to the job ads, and we crane over Veronique's shoulder. There are a couple jobs available, one for housecleaning and one for living in and minding some children while the parents are working.

Sometimes in these jobs we get paid in cash, sometimes only in food and a bed for the night. It's best to negotiate before you start the work, but really, when you're this hungry you're happy to work for a good meal, especially if there's some meat.

Veronique chooses the child minding job, which is closer and, if it lasts, will give her a place to sleep. The job is a good one; it pays $5.00 a month plus room and board. I hope she gets it. She's really too young to be sleeping in churches.

Cecile, who knows the city best, gives Veronique some directions and she starts at a fast walk, hoping to get there before another girl does. This would be a good job for Veronique, who likes children and took care of her younger sisters and brothers at home.

I go for the housecleaning job, which is on the other side of town, but I'm going to try for it anyway. I'm a fast walker.

I think about King Edward and Wallis Simpson as I walk and I'm not sure if it's a great love story or a great scandal. One thing I know for sure is that they aren't hungry like I am.

I wonder if I will ever have a great love. I'm 21 now, and if it weren't for the depression I would probably be thinking about beaus and getting married. But it is the depression, and I know I'm too scrawny to attract any man.

I increase my pace. I really want to get this job.

It takes about 40 minutes of walking . It's a large house in a nice section of town.

I knock on the door and the lady who answers is a large, kind- looking lady in a flowered dress, but she tells me that the job is already taken.

I must look exhausted and desperate because she tells me to come in to the kitchen and have a cup of tea before I start off again. Then she gives me a small piece of bread pudding, with a little maple syrup, and tea. The tea bag's been used a couple times already, so the tea is pretty weak, and I'm reminded that even people with money practice thrift. The pudding tastes wonderful. It's been a while since I've had anything besides coffee and doughnuts. I'm doing the dishes as a thank you gesture when the lady comes in.

"Are you going to be okay?" she asks me.

I can see she's sincerely concerned for me, and I assure her I'll be fine, and that the pudding was wonderful and really filling. We're both grateful to lie a bit, because we can't fix the situation anyway, and this lady's already been generous.

The only thing I can do now is go back and meet the others at our usual place. As I walk back I think about Amelia Earhart, and how she's flying a plane, and I can't even get enough to eat. But I really love that a woman is doing something that usually only men get to do.

I haven't had any kind of work for about two weeks now, and I start to feel discouraged for the first time. I know I'm losing weight, and I can see it in my friend's faces as well. And my hair is thinning out because I haven't had any protein for a long time.

Also, I don't get my monthlies very often.

We'll have to line up at the soup kitchen tonight, and this is something we hate because most of the people on the soup line are men, and sometimes they look at us in a bad way.

I see some women in the line-up now, and twice I've seen kids. I wonder about these kids, if they have a home and bed at night. I haven't yet seen any kids sleeping in the church, but I won't be surprised if that happens soon.

We'll certainly be back at the church tonight.

When I meet my friends back at our usual place, Veronique isn't there, so I guess she got the child minding job, and I feel really happy for her. I hope they treat her right. I hope she gets lots to eat.

Now there's only Denise, Cecile and me left to sleep in the church.

The soup lines don't open for another hour, so we walk down the sunny side of the street, looking at all the stuff we can't afford. We stay away from the restaurants because the smell of the food is too hard to take.

We look at the Butterick dress patterns in Eaton's window, and there's a new pattern for making a reversible house dress. I wish I was wearing one of those now, because this dress is showing the dirt, and it bothers me a lot, but I can't do anything about it.

Cecile is looking at the patterns for evening dresses. Her eyes shift to a mannequin dressed in a McCall pattern, then to bolts of material sitting where they won't get the sun on them: a brilliant blue, a red so dark it's almost black, a lemony yellow, and a deep plum.

And I see a different kind of hunger in Cecile's face.

"Green satin," she says to us. "Light-weight satin so it drapes well. That would be perfect."

I tell her I don't know. I've never had the chance to go to a dance or to a fancy restaurant. My life has been only work. I have the marks to prove it.

Denise glances at her sister, and then she puts her arm around Cecile's shoulder.

Cecile and Denise are from Quebec City, and they had a different kind of life than I had, but I don't really ask what happened. Some families that were rich lost everything. I guess that might be harder than starting out with nothing.

But I've never heard these girls say a word about how they used to live, or try to lord it over anyone because they had money before.

For some reason the two of them thought they would be more likely to get work here in Trois-Rivieres. It seems to me to be bad all over Quebec, but they've been here about 16 months now, a little longer than I have. It was them who told me I could sleep in the church.

I don't know why they came here instead of staying in Quebec City, but maybe it was so they wouldn't be seen by the girls they once went to parties with.

We walk past a store that has a radio in the window. It's playing loud big band music, and Denise and Cecile grab each other's hands and dance the jitterbug on the snowy sidewalk. Their skinny legs prance, the hem of their dresses flip up and down, and their braids bounce on their shoulders. A few people stop to smile.

Giggling, the three of us walk on to the soup line.

The line is long. I can smell fried bologna, and it smells wonderful. Someone rich must have made a donation. I hope we get some.

Someone in the lineup coughs, and everyone glances up. The threat of tuberculosis is always there. Consumption, some call it, and it kills.

The three of us are chatting about Veronique getting work, when I notice a man staring at Cecile.

"Hey, girlie," he says, loud enough to be heard by those around us. "You look pretty down on your luck. Tell you what: if I earn a dollar tomorrow, I'll meet you back here. You can do a little favour for me and I'll give you the dollar. I bet you'll like that."

A couple of the men laugh, but most of them scowl.

Denise and I get in front of Cecile to shield her, but the man continues to smirk as if he's said something clever.

"Arsehole," says Denise. Her voice is strong, full of contempt and unafraid, and the smirk drops from the man's face.

Cecile is close to tears, so we get out of line and go to the back. Now the wait will be longer, but we got away from that awful man.

When we get to the front of the line, the bologna is gone and the soup tastes mostly like water. There are a few vegetables in there, but they're so mushy we can't identify them.

"I never thought I'd be so glad to see a bit of cabbage," I say, trying to be cheerful.

Back at the church, before going to sleep, we play our favourite game: what we'll eat when we're rich. We detail meals rich with meat, warm bread and luscious desserts. Cecile talks about a chocolate pie her mother used to make with condensed milk.

Sometimes, I wonder if this is a smart thing to talk about when we're so hungry, and I switch the topic to Wallis Simpson, and whether she has committed mortal sin and will go to hell. The royal romance is interesting for a short while, but food is the only thing we think about these days, and we return to that topic.

Night falls, and we huddle in our coats and try to sleep, hoping the Depression will end soon, and hoping for work of some kind tomorrow.

My stomach grumbles.

Hunger Three

THE WORST THING FOR ME is that I can no longer help other people.

Now other people help me.

All my life I've taken care of others—my husband, my five daughters, my grandchildren. Sometimes it was difficult.

I never wanted to move out to the country but my husband insisted. He thought it would be healthier to raise the girls out in the clean air. In those days, wives did what their husbands said, so we moved. If I'd had my way we'd have stayed in the city, where I could visit my sisters-in-law and be able to get the groceries easily.

Of course, it was my life that got harder with the move, not Tom's. Well, the girl's lives changed too.

But me, I was the one who got all the extra work. It was me who heated up the water and poured it into the old galvanized tub to give my girls a bath on Saturday evenings. They had to be clean for church on Sunday. Well, that really only lasted a couple years. When the other babies came along, I made Tom get a bathtub inside, and that was a lot easier.

Today, I have a bath whenever I want to. I just need to tell the attendants. But that doesn't make up for the fact that my privacy is gone. Seems like it's now okay for anyone to see me without my clothes. I've gotten used to it somehow, and the attendants are mostly kind.

Getting old and being in this wheelchair is no fun. I can't walk anymore. And I can't read anymore. I went blind in my right eye about a year ago; I have some sight in my left eye, but it's going too. I can still recognize most people, but sometimes I recognize them by their voice or by what they're doing. When the doctor decided to find out why my right eye was starting to bulge out, he discovered a brain tumour. In one way, I'm glad my sight is going, because I can't even imagine how bad I look with my eye bulging out.

I've made a decision. It's still against the law to help anyone die, so I can't ask that of my girls. But it's not against the law for me to refuse food and water, and that's what I'm doing. After some fuss here, they offered me the palliative care room, which is bigger than my room, but I said no thanks. I want to die in my own room.

I seem to live a lot in the past now, and I'm dreaming of those old times again. I see that back room, the closet with all those old coats from the charity boxes, and my girls looking through the coats to find one that fits them for the winter. Sometimes, the sleeves were too short, and their mitts were short too, so they ended up with chilblains on their wrists. And with the dresses at their knees and their galoshes going only to their ankles, they were playing in the snow with half their legs bare. On really cold days, I insisted they wear their pajamas bottoms under their dresses when they went to school, and take them off before they went into class. It embarrassed them to be wearing pajamas to school, but I made them anyway. I don't know why they wouldn't let girls wear trousers to school in the winter. It was so old fashioned to insist on dresses all the time.

I got them their mitts and socks for Christmas, but there wasn't any money for coats.

I'm dreaming of long ago Christmases too. I mean Christmas with my girls, not when I was a kid in the orphanage. There was only one time when I wasn't able to get them something for Christmas. Like I said, I got them their socks, underwear, mitts, but nearly always a book each, and a board game for the family. Monopoly, Candy Land, Snakes and Ladders, Parcheesi. We had all of them.

And the girls had a collection of Hardy Boys and Nancy Drew books.

But that one time when I was in the hospital having my fourth daughter, there was just no money. When my daughters asked what they should say when the neighbourhood kids wanted to know what they got for Christmas, I told them to lie. Now ordinarily, I didn't approve of telling lies, but what were these kids going to say? It was too hard for them to say they got nothing. I know how that feels.

I had no idea what I was going to do when they got into high school. I didn't have any money for new clothes, and they would get made fun of for not being dressed like the other girls. And that's what happened. But they survived.

I'm cold now, and I know it's because I haven't eaten for a few days, and someone puts a warmed up blanket on me, and it feels good.

I remember that old house we lived in, and how cold it was. The windows were always frosted over, and the girls would melt the ice off the inside with the palm of their hand so they could see the mark they left on the windows. Other times, they just scratched off the frost so that they could look outside.

One of my daughters is here every day now. I know they're sad, but they figure it's my decision, except for the oldest one, who keeps on begging someone to do something, feed me with tubes or something. But the others tell her no, it's my decision.

Other people come too: my daughter's husbands and ex-husbands, and sometimes friends of my girls. And sometimes my grandchildren come.

When I first decided to stop food and water, I got hungry, but it wasn't terrible. I'm small now and don't eat much anyway. And it's not the first time I've been hungry.

But the hunger did make me think of those days during the depression when I was a young woman and had no money for food. Sometimes, if I couldn't get any work, I would go a full day with only a coffee and a doughnut. It made me think, too, of the times when I was trying to feed my family on very little. Potatoes, carrots, parsnips, those were the bases of many meals in the winter, with a little bit of meat cut up so small no one could find the pieces. Summer was better. Tom kept a garden, and when the neighbours went out, the girls got hold of some apples and strawberries.

I know it's the lack of water that will end it for me, and probably within this week. My daughters put some ice chips on my lips, and that feels good. My lips and skin are so dry. I would ask someone to put some cream on my face if I could find the energy to talk.

Today, there's someone else visiting me, but I don't recognize her. Well, like I said, I don't see too well anymore. My daughter tells me she was a childhood friend of hers when we lived out in the country and tells me her name is Cheryl, but I don't remember her at all. Cheryl says she wanted to see me and say thanks for helping her, and listening to her when she was a child. She gives a nervous laugh, and by that laugh I remember her.

As I drift off to sleep again, I remember turning the sheets. The sheets we had were so old and thin that I used to turn them side to middle. I cut them up the middle where they were very thin, and then sewed the outside edges together, where they were thicker, to make a new middle. They didn't tuck in at the sides anymore because they were too narrow, but they had to do. One of my daughters joked that it was a wonder all my girls didn't have seams up their backs from going to sleep on turned sheets.

Then Cheryl says thank you for the coat. And I remember.

She was just a little girl, and her coat was so, so thin. A hand-me-down from her brother, I think, but getting too small for her, and so worn out that I figured it did nothing to keep her warm. I had no coat for her. It was hard enough making sure my own kids were able to stay warm. I felt so bad for her, and really put my head into how I could help. And I did come up with something.

When the sheets had been turned lengthwise, and then width wise, and then worn out everywhere, I still saved them. Sometimes, I cut them up and hemmed them for drying the dishes; sometimes, I just used them for dusting. But I knew I had a large piece in the rag bag that I hadn't cut up yet. I pulled it out and folded it in four pieces, and hemmed the cut edges. Then I sewed that piece of sheet into the back of the coat, keeping it as square as I could. A little warmth for a little girl.

Somehow, thinking about that, about how Cheryl, all grown up, came to thank me for that little gift, made me feel settled.

I know my time is near. I hope no more memories come. I'm satisfied now that I did some good in the world, that I did some good for my family, which was both natural and my duty. But I did some good for others as well. I left something significant to mark my life.

I want to end with that last memory.

Acknowledgements

A special thank you goes to Isobel Raven and to Cynthia Robins for their excellent feedback, frequently provided under time restrictions, on many of my stories. Thank you to Shane Joseph for the opportunity to publish this collection, and for his feedback and suggestions.

Thank you also to all the Jolly Lits who have nourished my love of writing, and to others who encouraged me along the way.

Author Bio

Barb has loved reading and writing for as long as she can remember. She particularly likes the short story for its precision of language, for what is not said but only implied, and for the story's invitation to imagination.

Barb wrote the stories in this book over many years. The stories sometimes reflect her personal life experiences, and sometimes reflect the life experiences of friends and strangers. Many of them grew out of randomly overheard stories, others are pure imagination.

Barb grew up in a very rural Ontario area, and attended a one room school house with a very outdated selection of books. Consequently she read many of the classics. When she was in the middle of grade eight a new two-room school was constructed, and she was overjoyed to have the use of an inside bathroom.

As an avid reader Barb knew there was a more exciting life to come, and she was right. Whatever she can't do herself, her characters can do.

Barb moved to Toronto at the age of 18, eventually became a social worker, and worked for the City of Toronto. She retired in 2010, and loves retirement, and the freedom to travel, kick box, lift weights, and drink lots of coffee with friends. She is pleased to have time to spend with her granddaughter, and delighted that she is finally getting enough sleep.

Printed in the USA
CPSIA information can be obtained
at www.ICGtesting.com
LVHW022156141123
763979LV00034B/727